Heaven & Hell

Heaven & Hell

Gawain Barker

ISBN-13: 978-1-7642282-0-6

Cover design and imprint
bushbrother

website
thecolourofshadows.com

Real Cheeky – 1
Something Else – 10
By Golly – 19
The Antidote – 29
Better Than the Movie – 45
Suntory Cowboy – 72
The Big Picture – 85
Dr Tarzan, I Presume – 97
The Elephant –112
Molecules of Light – 129
No Whys or Hows – 146
White Rabbit –160
Heaven & Hell – 180
Passing As Men – 189
Shark Bait – 199
Good As – 223

Real Cheeky

Despite the ceiling fans whirring away, it was muggy and hot inside the wooden church. Down the back, Seth mouthed words to hymns he didn't know. Three rows up was the bloke he was going to bash.

The bastard had seen him as he'd gone down the aisle, following what looked like his mum, dad and sister, and the look of shock on his face was right on the money. Showed he was guilty.

Seth could have waited outside, but he wanted to be real cheeky. When the story got around town about how he'd turned up in church to get his man, blokes would think a little differently about him, and he didn't mind that.

With eyes slanted sideways, he sneaked a peek at the pretty young thing across the aisle: straight-backed, pink-cheeked, sweat darkening the armholes of her sleeveless dress. Someone's daughter, she'd break some fella's heart.

From three rows up came the flash of a face checking to see if the big blonde bastard was still there. I sure am, thought Seth. You keep on singing, mate, and we'll see how you do outside.

Rory Wales seemed normal enough. No wife or kids, he took his oldies to church on Sunday and welded steel for a living. A tank playing footy, he wasn't scared of a blue.

Seth felt a mixture of glee and trepidation at what was coming. He'd seen Rory fight before: one steamy night by the railway tracks outside the National Hotel.

With the bang of cane bins unloading down Spence Street and the fruit bats screeching in the tree across the tracks, Rory had slugged it out with a big fella, the two contestants cheered on by the contents of the front bar.

He'd easily biffed the fella about, knocking sweat flying, blows thudding into flesh and bone, but the bloke had a mate who joined in. Rory had to step it up, and he did; the first fella took a beauty to the jaw and went down. The mate hoed in, and Rory began smacking him around, but this bastard also had a mate, who, to the delight of the yelling mob, jumped in.

Swerving and dodging, the men grunted as they traded punches. It was hot work, but Rory played competition footy and wasn't even close to puffed yet. Dodging in close to mate number two, he feinted, tackled, and flattened him. Up on his feet in a flash, he went for mate number one again, and this fella, seeing his chums on their bums, took off down the railway track into the night. There was an eruption of cheers and laughter, and under the star-spangled sky, Rory raised his hands like he was holding a trophy.

Seeing him fight alone was a rare thing, as Rory had a little mob of mates, fellas he played footy with. They got unruly at times, but only with other unruly blokes, and that was something good you could say about Rory, because in the keep-your-hands-to-yourself department, he'd fallen down big time, nicking a swag of dough from a well-liked bloke. Now some retribution was in order.

But first there were hymns and the sermon, and Seth prayed for time to speed by. Around him, women fanned themselves, and fellas' brows shone with sweat. You must really have to believe the bull to put yourself through this, he thought. It was the deadliest, dreariest thing he could imagine: the out-of-tune voices, the droning waffle of the sermon, and the fidgeting people coughing and sighing, while a bloke in a dress up the front tried to make you feel guilty about something.

Back in sixth grade he'd wholeheartedly supported his brother's revolt at having to go to church, both of them over the mumbo jumbo. Mum was furious, but Dad didn't really care. Church for him was a social thing, and he'd soothed her into acceptance.

The only thing Dad ever said about religion and all that was that prayer had got him through some evil times, and Seth knew that he meant the war in New Guinea.

When the service finished, everyone moved in a rumble of shoes on the timber floor. One of the first outside, Seth went to the line of cars parked along the street and turned to watch the door. The church emptied, groups of people stopping to have a chat, but no Rory Wales.

Seth moved along behind the cars into the broken shade of a flame tree and stood watching the straight, normal citizens of Cairns having their Sunday catch-up. This mob has no idea about what's really going on, he thought.

"You, Kelly," said a voice like God. Turning, Seth saw someone he'd known since he'd been a toddler going arse-up on the Esplanade mudflats.

Des Drysdale was an old family acquaintance and a real churchie. He'd given Seth some boxing lessons ten years ago, even coming to a few of his bouts. A fit old bastard then and probably eighty now, he still stood tall.

"G'day, Mr. Drysdale," said Seth.

"In church, son?" The old bloke didn't hide his surprise. Seth nodded.

"This church, Kelly? It's not Catholic."

"No harm in hedging your bets, Mr. Drysdale."

That didn't go down so well. Drysdale's hard little eyes shone with anger. Wounded beyond marriage in the Great War, he was a man close to God, who'd as soon deliver a sermon as talk.

"Faith is to be taken seriously," he boomed. "It's not to be knocked and made fun of."

Heads turned, faces smiled. Old Man Drysdale was still giving young blokes what for.

"Sorry, Mr. Drysdale," said Seth. "I was being a goose."

Drysdale frowned mightily. He wasn't wearing a dress, but he was sure as hell trying to make Seth feel bad.

C'mon, you old bastard, thought Seth. It was a joke.

"Yeah, my mate was supposed to be here," he said. "I went inside to look, the service started, and I just stayed."

Drysdale grunted in surprise, then gave Seth some Old Testament eyes. "You feel something in there, boy?"

Seth nodded faintly. "Yeah, I dunno. It was a bit hot . . . but it was alright, aye."

"Well, that's grand you like our church. You're welcome any time."

"Thank you, Mr. Drysdale," said Seth.

"Keeping out of trouble?" said Drysdale. "Keeping it in the ring and not on the street?"

"Yeah, mostly." Seth put up his hands like they were an

exhibit in court. "But in my job as a doorman, I've got to use them sometimes. The public can be a tricky beast."

"The only beast to worry about is the one inside you."

Standing there with the old bastard preaching at him, with churchies all around, Seth felt that split in reality: a dislocation from how things had always been and where they were going. It was 1974 now, and young people knew the score. The cool ones, that is. But far north Queensland was still so far behind the times.

And old Drysdale here was the far north incarnate. He'd grown up without electricity, or anything really, and he believed what the papers and TV and the government told him. And he read the good book every day.

He didn't know about the rush of rock'n'roll and fast cars. He'd never got loaded on rum and marijuana and danced and rooted with up-for-it chicks while Cactus or Buffalo rocked from the speakers at a party that went all weekend. It would crack his head wide open.

Bunging it on, Seth looked reflective.

"Well, if I use more force than necessary, it's because the bloke needs to be taught a lesson and gets punished. It's what God would do, right, Mr. Drysdale?"

The old bloke spluttered with outrage.

"Don't be so arrogant! You cannot compare yourself to him! You can't imagine what *he* might do. You can't wield that power. Judgement and punishment are not for you to employ. You said you work as a doorman?"

Seth nodded.

"You are in the *service* of the public. You are there to protect people – and that's all. You're a handy fighter, boy, but don't let the Devil guide your fists. Otherwise, you'll find out that in jail there's a never-ending line of blokes ready to knock you flat."

"I know that, Mr. Drysdale."

Drysdale looked taken aback. "You've been to prison?"

"Oh, no, Mr. Drysdale, I just . . . know that blokes who like fighting often end up in jail."

The old bloke snorted. A face appeared at a window in the church and looked out. Rory. He must be feeling a bit nervous, and Seth liked that. It was good to be dominant from the get-go.

Drysdale's tone changed. With a gesture of his hand, he said, "Look at this. Good people gathered at the church talking, a peaceful Sunday with blue skies over our little town. Even a flock of angels."

In a bush on the other side of the road, lorikeets were noisily eating. "Is this not heaven?" said Drysdale.

Seth couldn't see it. It was just another hot, small-town Sunday. The lassitude must have shown on his face, and the old bloke's face hardened.

"You don't know how hard this world can be, boy."

Didn't every old bloke say that? thought Seth. And how they'd all had it so much tougher back in the day?

"Yeah, I 'spose," he conceded. "Cairns is alright."

"No, no." Drysdale's eyes pinned him. "You cannot be careless about this. Look at the beauty and peace around you. You don't know how desperate things can really get."

Seth knew he was talking about the Great War.

"You don't know hell," said Drysdale, with real doom in his voice. "Or how quickly we can get there."

"Well, if I keep going to church, I never will, right, Mr. Drysdale?"

The old churchie's face reddened.

Jesus, thought Seth, he's touchier than a lawn full of sensitive weed. Looking past him, Seth saw that Rory had come outside. The sister was leading Mum and Dad to a blue Morris, and that was good. The bastard's parents had been an unwelcome surprise. Now he'd wait by Rory's car, a nice red Monaro he'd seen him arrive in earlier.

"You mock with ill intent!" Drysdale was firing up.

"I've got to go now, Mr. Drysdale. You have a good day."

"Do not choose that path, Kelly. It goes to hell."

With an impudent smile, Seth went onto the street and began walking along the row of cars in the direction of the Monaro. It was time for business now. Putting a scare into the bloke wasn't enough. The bastard had a bill to pay.

It was sad, because Rory wasn't really a bad bloke. But he'd pooed on his plate, stealing money from a mate of everybody's. He'd even been to the bloke's house and sat there having a beer with him. He'd been trusted, and then he'd done this. It was a bad show alright.

"Oi! Oi, you bastard!"

Seth stopped by a Land Rover and turned. Rory was coming up the street at a trot, his face stiff with anger.

"What in the blue fuckeroo are you doing here? With my parents here! In church!"

"They've got nothing to do with this," said Seth. "I heard you were a churchie, but I didn't know they'd be here."

"That's the *only* reason I'm here," said Rory, and Seth saw his rage drop to just really pissed-off.

"Who in hell is telling you to come after me?" said Rory. "You ask around first? You smart enough to do that?"

"You did something wrong," said Seth.

"Something wrong? Yeah, don't tell me – I stole some money from Ricky Squires. Two thousand bucks, right?"

"You sure did. Now you have to make restitution."

"Restitution? What for? I'm no bloody thief."

"It won't take long. Five seconds tops. C'mon, let's go to your car. You can sit in it afterwards," said Seth.

Rory's face suffused with blood.

"Bugger you! What sort of dog on a lead do you think I am?"

"A mongrel one that needs to be taught a lesson."

"What about if I tell you to shove it up your arse?"

Seth monstered him with a lazy smile. "I'll shove it right back." Rory shook his head in amazement.

"You really are a dumb bastard."

"Let's go to your car, mate," said Seth.

Rory frowned and stepped forward, his fists coming up. Seth backed down between the Land Rover and an Austin Freeway.

"Where you going?" sneered Rory.

"Well, if you're going to make a blue of it, let's not scare the oldies, hey?"

"My oath, I'm going to make a blue of it," said Rory.

He strode in between the two vehicles, and in the cover of the Land Rover's cabin, they closed in a flurry of solid punches. They went hard. Shoulders and arms soaked up big fists and nuts-and-bolts knuckles, but no-one went for the head. Not yet anyhow.

Then Seth got the jump on the bastard, knocked him into the Land Rover, and drove a punishment fist into his solar plexus. Flipping over like a rag doll, Rory writhed against dusty metal, his lungs silently crying for oxygen.

Seth moved in, calculating how much more retribution to exact. A couple of broken ribs should do it.

"Hey! Hey you, Kelly!"

Seth looked around and saw Des Drysdale barrelling down between the vehicles, his face crimson, his lumpy fists like clubs.

"You rotten little bastard," snarled Drysdale.

He thudded a blow into Seth's outstretched arm, then glanced a good punch off his chest. In disbelief, Seth tried to stay in the cover of the Land Rover and defend himself without fighting back. It was hard work, as the old bastard went for it like it was the last chance he'd ever have to get stuck into a bloke.

Backpedalling, Seth came out onto the road. Drysdale, suddenly out of wind, leant with one hand on the side of the Land Rover and bared his teeth.

"You truck with Satan, boy," he growled.

"He deserved it," said Seth.

"Didn't I just tell you? It's not for you to judge! And not for you to punish!"

Seth looked around for watching faces, but no one had seen the biffo. Frustrated as hell, he began to quickly walk to his truck, parked on the next block over.

A yell rang out. Rory had got his breath back.

"You bloody idiot! You're out in the desert on a boat with this one."

Something Else

"What? Do you like having to hit blokes?" said Walter. "Mate, finding you working here is no real surprise, but I can't think of a worse way to make a quid."

"Ah, it's not so bad," grinned Seth. "Rock'n'roll, chicks, and I get to see what's happening around Cairns at night."

In a pressed white shirt, black pants, and black leather shoes, Seth stood by the entrance to the Windsor Room. It was warm enough, the air close and damp, and from Lake Street came the revving V8 engines and yells of a Saturday night. Through the door behind him came the thump of rock'n'roll. Inside, dinner was nearly done, and popular local band Coppersole was beginning to turn it up with their second set of the night.

"You still surveying?" said Seth.

"Too right I am," said Walter. "Doing geo samples, too. Sometimes I have three blokes on the go. I'm picking up a load of good work, Seth."

"Well, good for you, mate." Seth meant it, but he saw the rugged miles out west: the dust and heat, the endless eucalyptus, and hard rocky hills. He'd worked with Walter before.

"They got me a new truck, pay for fuel *and* tucker, and the money's real good." Walter was spruiking it to him.

"That's bloody great," said Seth, pleased his mate was doing alright. The bloke was a bit older than him, and he'd done it tough, with violence and sickness claiming loved ones and family. He was a solid bloke, honest and fair, and that had made him the white sheep of the family. But Walter knew how to have his fun.

"Where did you come from?" said Seth. "Out west?"

"Nah, I just finished up a job on Hinchinbrook Island for Department of Lands. Wasn't so easy. Some hard country, fierce bloody insects, and a bit of rain. But we had a bonza time. You been there?"

Seth shook his head. He'd seen it from the ocean.

"You should, mate," said Walter. "It's something else. Animals are all big, like in a movie. Spider, goanna, snake, they all bloody big, hey. You look at solid rock mountains sticking up like teeth in the sky, and there's swamps, bays, cliffs, beaches, waterfalls – you bloody name it. Rugged as a bastard, but wunderbar."

"We sailed past but never went ashore," said Seth, his memory flashing on the beach he'd seen from a boat when he'd been twelve: a long, bright strip of sand completely dwarfed by sunlit jungle and a great wall of sheer peaks.

That remote and wild scene had stayed with him over the years; a vision of mystery that had become the stuff of dreams. Hinchinbrook Island always looked fascinating from the Bruce Highway, but never like that.

"It's the land that time forgot," said Walter. "And good bloody fishing. Take a lot of ice. You'll love it, mate."

"It's on my list," said Seth. "I'll borrow a boat."

"You do that. So what's it like inside? Any goers?"

Seth smiled and opened the door. "Get stuck in, mate."

Walter winked and went in. The smile stayed on Seth's face. Yeah, that was another good thing about working on door – you got to catch up with old mates.

Folding his arms across his chest, he glanced at the Rolex Submariner on his wrist. Five past nine. It was a big contrast to a few months ago when he'd been deep in the scrub growing a marijuana crop. Up there he'd be asleep an hour after sunset, then up at dawn.

He looked at the group of men and women smoking and talking where the alley from Lake Street opened into an undercover car park. He recognised quite a few of them.

There were the regular night owls: fellas in good shirts and slacks, the chicks in party frocks, mascara, and lippie; a bloke he'd refused entry last week, sober tonight; and Nancy the nurse, who he'd got in the sack with last year. Their eyes met, and he wondered if she might be up for it later when he knocked off.

Meeting chicks was the best perk of the job, and he usually did well there. He wasn't the ugliest bloke around; some women said he was quite the looker, plus he was friendly and funny, and they always liked that.

And there he was – the fella who hadn't come up to the door yet. Reasonably well-dressed, loitering and smoking cigarettes in the car park, only coming into the light to check his watch like he was waiting for someone. It looked like bullshit to Seth.

In a boom of music, a woman came out of the door. Seth smiled politely, got a tired smile in return. She passed the mob of talkers, and the smoker came out of the shadows and went up to her. He smiled around a stream of words, but his patter flopped, and the woman didn't stop. The bloke began moving with her, said something, and she recoiled in disgust. As she stormed away, the bastard spat onto her skirt. She didn't notice, but Seth sure had.

Quick smart he made for them. The woman picked up speed, her footsteps echoing over the hubbub of voices. A couple of chicks turned as Seth went past the crowd.

The grinning prick now saw him coming, and an arse-licker of a grin wet his lips, his eyes going, 'Haven't we all dealt with a smart-arse chick like that before?'

Seth felt righteous adrenaline pumping. He wanted to move the filthy grub's nose right across his face with his fist. Instead, using his body to shield the action from view, he threw a blur of a punch at the man's face, pulling back an inch from his snoot.

Shocked, the bastard recoiled. Seth crowded forward, zapping in another harmless blow, and the grub hopped backwards. At the end of the alley, Seth saw the woman hit the street. She turned out of sight, and some people came in, making for the Windsor Room.

With his back to the crowd, Seth pushed the bastard up against the wall and saw that his clothes were not so flash after all.

"These people will go past first," he said, monstering him with an evil stare. The bastard began to protest, but Seth growled him down.

"Behave, or I really will hit you. And hard too."

Wide-eyed, the grub digested this. Seth nodded in grim encouragement as the people came up.

Two blokes and a chick, young, well-dressed enough, and a little pissed. They nodded as they passed, their attention on the muffled thump of the rock'n' roll ahead.

Seth didn't move. Unsure, the grub waited until music came out of the open door, then he pushed off the wall, his stupid face wracked with protest.

"What do you think you're doing?" he said.

"You dirty bastard," said Seth, his hands in view by his sides. "You are now barred from here."

"I didn't touch her. Not a finger."

Very fast, Seth spun him around to face Lake Street. He discreetly kneed him in the bum while pointing his arm up the alley. "Move your arse."

Hands still in view, Seth moved him forward with more knee jabs, everything hidden by his body. As he corralled the grub forward, he looked with longing at the back of his head. Lucky for you I'm at work, he thought.

On the street, Mr. Spits turned, his dirty mouth opening to speak. Seth ran at him, and the grub took off down Lake Street in the direction of the Barbary Coast.

Going to the kerb, Seth looked past him, scanning both sides of the street. He turned and checked the other end and was relieved that the woman was nowhere to be seen. Get home safe, love, he thought.

Back up the alley, faces turned towards him. A couple of girls were smiling; a bloke raised a hand in salute. Seth nodded back and took his place at the door. That was another cool thing about the job: fellas' esteem at his ability to sort things out. Maybe he should give lessons.

Congratulating himself on not giving in to awful joy and smashing the grub, he began to give his shirt a good once-over, looking for spit. Music blared as the door opened, and an avian cry of hilarity stabbed him in the ear.

"Dear God, what's on your shirt now?" yelled Evan.

The bouncer passed Seth and turned to look. He shook his head. "I've never known a bloke in this game to be so fussy about his clobber."

"Ah, this dirty bastard was spitting."

The bouncer's eyebrows shot up in revulsion.

"He won't be back," said Seth.

"You biff him?" said Evan.

"Nah, I don't want to hit a bloke in the back of the head until I have to," said Seth.

"Fair enough." Evan knew all about temptation.

Wide-shouldered and stocky, he also knew about hard yakka, busting muscle in breweries and on building sites since he was a teen. Now in his late forties, he was happy working doors. Nothing like real work, he'd say.

He was as ugly as real sin, and along the way someone had also broken his nose. Easy-going and steady when it mattered, he'd probably kicked fellas on the ground and broken a dozen arms and legs, but he was a good bloke to work with.

"Remember that boxer?" said Seth.

"Aye? A boxer?" Evan's brow wrinkled; he shot Seth a doubtful look. "What bloody boxer?"

"The boxer. A few months ago. The Sydney bloke."

Remembering now, Evan cackled loudly. He sounded like a mad bird, and that always made Seth smile.

"Aw yeah, that bloke – the boxer," said Evan. "What was his name? Told us he was a champion boxer. Who was he? Won some state title?"

"I didn't hear, aye," said Seth.

"He sure big-mouthed himself."

A couple of blokes, smokes in mouth, listened in.

"Got chopped down," said Evan. "Like a bloody tree."

He nodded happily at the memory.

"We were standing right here, and the sheila with him

screams like a tiger, then bloody moves like one, and he goes down holding his nuts. Christ almighty! The sound his head made on the concrete. Out like a fuckin' light."

"Don't take your eyes off your man, hey?"

"She sure fuckin' didn't."

"What was his name again?" said Seth, just to hear the bouncer's screech of a laugh.

From inside, the music ended, the band taking a break. Evan and Seth moved away from the door. Seconds later people poured outside to talk and smoke cigarettes, and the two bouncers stood watching them. A good few of the crowd were drunk, but no one was playing up yet.

Evan went back in, and Seth thought about Mr. Spits and the fine line he walked in this job. It was inevitable that someone got a touch-up now and then: fellas whose sense of reason had been swamped by grog, or by the urge to show off to mates, or by the simple thrill of punching a bloke as he tried to punch you. Seth knew about that one.

And, as sad as wet bread, were the unseeing alcoholics who fought their monsters through you. You sorta felt sorry for blokes like that. But you still hit 'em.

He avoided fighting, usually defusing trouble with talk or with the judicious use of force, blocking and pushing people. Punching punters was for special circumstances, when the public, and, most importantly, himself, were at risk of being hurt.

That kind of dangerous violence needed to be stopped, and stopped fast. But get it wrong, and things could end up in hospital and in court. He'd seen a few shockers, door gorillas destroying fellas for no proper reason, but the bastards he decked always had it coming.

An hour later, with the band into their next set, some blokes came down the alley and approached Seth: three Aboriginal fellas in their mid-twenties, dressed alright in long-sleeved shirts, clean jeans, and buffed cowdy boots. One bloke had a lit smoke in his mouth.

They all caught his eye, anxious determination on their faces. These fellas wanted beer and rock'n'roll, and maybe a few rums. They all looked fit as fiddles, like they'd been working out west with cattle or on the railway.

Turning to one side, Seth smiled with the doorman's welcome: something like being the host for the night, but totally in charge. He opened the door, nodded to them. A chick's nervy titter came from the group talking, and a few faces turned to watch like it was the strangest thing in the world.

Stoney-faced, the three blokes quickly passed, smelling of cigarettes, beer, and wood smoke. "Cheers, mate," said one bloke tonelessly.

Pulling the door closed, Seth heard laughter. People were watching him, with two blokes giving him the hard eye. As per the job, he ignored them.

A few minutes later the three Aboriginal blokes came out the door, one swearing hard. They brushed past Seth.

"Hey," said Seth. "What's happening?"

"Why'd you even bother?" said one bloke. "Waste our bloody time! We'll go somewhere where our money's the same colour as everyone else's."

The two hard-eyed bastards in the mob of talkers made cries of mock disappointment, and people laughed. Evan was suddenly at Seth's shoulder, and they watched the three fellas stride off up to Lake Street.

"Yeah, Kevvy didn't like that," said Evan.

"Hey Evan," yelled one of the bastards. "You need to bring him up to speed, mate."

Evan ignored them. Seth breathed nice and slow, and the two bastards laughed again, their voices basso with pleasure. The two bouncers stood there in silence, then with a boom of music, Kevvy, the night manager, came out. He closed the door, checked out the crowd, and then looked at Seth.

"Yeah, not tonight, mate." He was sweating from the crush inside.

"Is there a special night then?" said Seth. Evan grunted unhappily. Kevvy stared at Seth, then appeared to make his mind up.

"Or any other night."

"Just *those* three blokes, right?"

"Don't be a fuckin' smartarse," said Kevvy, and he went back inside.

"What are you doing, mate?" said Evan. "You're not Mr. Irreplaceable, y'know."

"Ahh, it's bullshit," said Seth. "They were presentable, they weren't drunk, and their money's the same colour as everyone else's, right?"

Evan pursed his lips. "Yeah, well, you're probably right, but you don't want to be pissing him off."

There really wasn't much to say after that, and Evan went back inside. With a tight smile at the ready, Seth stood at his post and waited for the anger to drain away.

By Golly

Around eleven, the first real trouble of the night came swaggering down the alley: three blokes in nice gear, the best-dressed one taking the lead. Seth recognised him: a short-arse, rich kid, apparently pissed off at having to work in the family business. The poor little bastard.

Seth had let him through the door of a couple of venues in town before, and he'd behaved himself, but right now he could see the signs – the slack-eyed look that passed for toughness and the jerky, self-conscious movements betraying the anticipation of starting something, with his two stupid mates acting just the same.

As the trio came up, some fella called out to Richie Rich, and he yelled a greeting back. The two hard-eyed bastards smiled, nodding at this exchange, a few other blokes too.

From the countless hours he'd spent watching people in loud venues, Seth had got fairly handy at lip-reading, and he saw Richie Rich mutter to his mates, "Look at this cunt. Thinks he's tough." Not *think*, thought Seth.

At the door, it was obvious they'd been on the grog. The combination of inebriation with their biff-ready strutting was going to be a problem. Inside the venue, they'd bump about in the crowded room, knocking drinks, squashing up against tits and bums, and inevitably, fists would fly.

"Sorry, boys," said Seth with a ringmaster's smile. "It's pretty full in there, and, well . . . so are you fellas."

"The fuck we are," said one bloke.

"Language, mate. Please," said Seth evenly. The rich kid came in close, stinking of cologne, cigarettes, and grog.

"Don't piss us around. I know the owner," he said.

"Good for you," said Seth, "but right now you and your mates are too intoxicated to enter the premises. If any of you come a gutser in there, then your mate, the owner, will be liable. And so will I. So, c'mon fellas, turn around and go back the way you came."

The idiots began swearing and crowding in. Seth took a big step back and held out his arms as a barrier.

"Let's be clear, gents – you're not coming in." Seth saw the urge to violence cloud their eyes, the old three against one making it possible. But they knew he was big game, and he didn't think they really wanted to risk a cracked jaw or black eye.

"Please, fellas," said Seth, loud enough for everyone to hear. "You've had a big night. Go home, and have a rum for me when you get there. Okay?"

"Nah, nah, nah," said Richie Rich, coming right up.

"Stop," said Seth in cold command. With the door at his back, he calmly reached out to move the idiot back – and saw him suddenly transfer his weight to his left side. It was too close for a real punch, and Seth looked down and saw the bastard's right leg jerking up. Madly twisting, he yanked his thigh around, felt a knee punch into muscle. It hurt, and there was going to be a good bruise tomorrow – but his balls were okay.

Grabbing Richie Rich, he resisted the urge to fire a goal kick into the prick's nuts. Using his belt and collar, Seth flipped him horizontal, then used him to bulldoze his two mates back up the alley.

Squawking in shock, the two clowns backpedalled, their leader yapping and squirming. Seth went hard, and the giddy twits had to turn and run. Keeping up, he jammed Richie Rich's bleating face into their arses.

Shoes scraped madly, and Seth felt through the body he was holding one of the stampeding men stumble. Pulling back a bit, he let the bastard stay on his feet, then smashed Richie Rich back into the fray and ran them all out onto Lake Street.

Whacking the nasty little turd down, Seth pushed him against a Holden panel van. Spittle ran from a corner of the bastard's mouth. Yuck, thought Seth, disgusted by the sight. I hope I don't have to bleach my shirt.

A few metres away on the sidewalk, the other two one-carton heroes stopped and looked around for their leader. Richie Rich was trying to maintain his balance, the night's drinking and surprise aeroplane ride turning him green. Seth looked him up and down: one shoe was a bit scuffed, but he didn't look anything close to roughed-up.

Seth quickly stepped back as the bastard began spitting onto the footpath. He gave him the solid steel eyes.

"That's a taste of what bouncers will do to you if you try to knee 'em in the balls. Alright? Now piss off, and don't ever come back."

Richie Rich slithered off the car and threw up. Seth strode back up the alley, mission accomplished, in what – forty seconds?

Just about everyone was watching him as he went to the door. Chicks talking and smoking followed him with their eyes. Blokes gave him long looks and blank stares. He felt like a panther at a zoo.

A woman's voice cut through the talk, directed at him.

"Where do you get off on hurting people, mate?"

"Yeah, you fuckin' thug," yelled a bloke. "He isn't just anyone!"

Seth stopped. The crowd fell silent.

"He tried to assault me. I picked him up, as you all saw, and on the street I put him down, on his feet, and without a scratch. He didn't get hurt. I didn't get hurt. Alright?"

With a bland smile, he took up his position at the door again. Conversations resumed, but he could tell by the angry glances and excited faces that they were about him. He didn't mind. That's how reputations were made.

With his eyes in the middle distance, he listened to the room behind him, the energy peaking. Inside everyone would be going off, fully charged on hours of drinking. He was glad he'd sent those idiots packing.

There now came a shortage of idiots, and that was fine with him. Half an hour later, Evan came out. Turning his back to the talking mob, he held out two fifties at waist height.

"What's that for, mate?" said Seth.

"Your pay," said Evan.

Seth got it, but he didn't like it.

"The rich kid?"

"Yep. His father rang up, boiling mad. Cairns is a small town. You wanna keep it on a chain, mate."

"Well, that's real nice, isn't it?" said Seth. "His nasty little son tried to knee me in the nuts so that his drunk mates could jump up and down on my head."

"Is that right?" Evan's eyes went cold. Seth nodded. The bouncer sighed and shook his head at the injustice of it.

"Mate, it's not my decision. I wish it was. Management, y'know. They don't really care about what we have to deal with out here."

Evan shook the money. Seth took it and slid it into his pocket. Evan stuck out his hand. Without menace, his eyes said, *now go*.

"Been good working with ya," he said.

"Same here, mate," said Seth, and they shook hands.

Evan nodded goodbye and went back in. Seth took a deep breath, then saw those two arseholes watching him. From their faces, he could see that they were working out what they'd just seen. Sure enough, as he passed by, one of them called out.

"See? Never too big to get chopped down to size. You and your fuckin' black mates got too big for your boots."

Technically, Seth wasn't working anymore. He could give this shitbox a go; pull him apart in front of everyone. But it was the wrong time and place to give out a hiding. Sacked or not, it didn't feel professional.

He amiably nodded at the glaring blokes and wide-eyed girls, reserving a hard look for the mouthy prick. Then some fellas jeered. He stopped, and they all shut up.

"You try doing that. Any of you," he said, pointing at the door of the Windsor Room. "How long you reckon you'd be cool and dandy with it? Spit flying, bastards trying to knee you in the balls, every drunk idiot wanting to fight you. How long you reckon you'd last – just having to take it, night after night?"

He dug the looks some of the chicks were giving him.

"No, that was actually perfect timing. They put me out of my misery before I put someone out of theirs."

Laughing loudly at their silence, he went up the alley to his car on Lake Street.

Not yet ready to go back home with his tail between his legs, Seth drove out of town towards the range. With the windows open and his head half out, he relished the air. He sure needed a drink, and he drove away from town and up to where lights sparkled in the darkness – up to the House on the Hill.

The two-storey timber building had been a commando training base in the war for missions behind enemy lines. Seth could scarcely imagine the guts they must have had. They'd even attacked ships in Singapore Harbor in fold-up canoes. Many had died in action, some executed by the Japs. Forget the hard-nuts I know, he thought. Those Z-Force boys were the real tough guys.

Back when he was a teen, the place, known as Fairview, had got run down, and kids would dare each other to go up to the building. He'd seen a few things there, and he'd never forgotten that afternoon when he was fifteen.

Then a few years ago the place had been done up real nice with a bandstand and dance floor, bars, a restaurant, and a few air-conditioned units to stay overnight in. It had caught on like a house on fire, and what with weddings, events, and parties, drink specials and dancing to local and out of town bands, it really rocked up at the House on the Hill.

He pulled into the car park. There were vehicles and a few people standing at the foot of the stairs that went to the second floor. He probably had an hour or so before it closed, enough to get a few drinks in and, if he was lucky, find a nice bit of fluff to leave with.

A band was playing a Sherbet cover, a bit sad really, but that went with the territory. Often the bands would wear matching shirts and strides, silly bloody uniforms that real rock groups never wore.

He knew the difference. Since his early teens, he'd been buying records, and he'd caught most of the good bands that made it to Cairns. He'd travelled to Brisbane a few times to see bands from overseas, including Led bloody Zep, who were just about the best thing he'd ever seen.

Yeah, he'd seen enough to know who the wild ones were, the real rock'n'rollers who meant it, and not just an 'act' with an album to push.

As he got out, he smelt vomit. He looked at his feet, let his eyes adjust. He wasn't walking in someone's dinner if he could help it, and he went carefully across the car park. Upstairs he got a rum and coke at the bar – and suddenly felt tired.

He thought of the sweltering Queenslander house on Digger Street that he shared with Gary Sparks, the boys drinking carton after carton of beer and talking rubbish, the stereo way up, the fridge empty, and the dunny paper all used. He took a consoling hit of his drink.

Living with Gary was cheap and friendly, but it was like high school camp, but with booze and drugs. It was junior and mundane, and he was over it. He wanted to wake up somewhere different, somewhere interesting: some place where he knew nobody and no one knew him.

Finishing his drink, he ordered another. As he waited, he stared at the bottles behind the bar. It wasn't just his living arrangements he was done with; it was everything. He wanted to be somewhere where he wasn't subjected to demeaning stuff like what had happened tonight and where he wasn't expected to do grubby things like last Sunday. Yeah, the bastard who'd said it was right – hell was other people.

"Good evening, mate." A voice at his shoulder, the tone polite but forceful: just the sort of voice he'd use working doors. He turned, and sure enough, two bouncers were standing by the bar in white shirts and black pants. Seth recognised one of them: Lex Tickles. He'd worked with him a couple of times. Lex got his moniker from how hard he hit blokes.

"G'day, Lex," said Seth.

He didn't know the other bloke, the bastard built like an ox and not looking much smarter than one. The big twit gave off the distinct impression that he wanted something to happen. Very unprofessional. Then Seth twigged that Lex must have given him the drum on who this big blonde bastard was. Sometimes having a rep wasn't so good.

Seth waited for Lex to acknowledge him, to say hello like a good sport, but it was like the bastard didn't know him anymore. It was bloody odd, and some blokes at the bar turned to watch.

"I'm going to have to ask you to leave," said Lex. His face was a blank, but at the back of his eyes there was a sort of 'howzat, I caught you out' look.

"Why's that, mate?" said Seth amiably.

Lex nodded at Seth's shirt and trousers.

"No work clothes. You wanna go home and get cleaned up before coming in here. People are having a nice night out. You don't want to be spoiling it for them."

"Are you serious?" said Seth. "Mate, I'm just having a knock-off drink. I'm dressed just like you blokes."

Lex looked pointedly at something on Seth's shirt, his eyes triumphantly disgusted.

"I don't think so. Have a look at that."

Seth twisted, craned his neck, looked, and Jesus! In the folds of his shirt, just above where it was tucked into the waistband, he saw a wet, encrusted stain, and his skin crawled at the horrible filthiness of it. Richie Rich had spewed on him while he was getting his plane ride.

"Mate, it's been a hard night," he said, tucking his shirt in and trying not to think about what was now touching his skin.

"Yeah, tell us about it," said Lex, and he motioned for Seth to get up. The Ox sniffed the tainted air, made a hard face. Seth felt a blinding white light go off in his skull.

Then the second drink arrived. The Ox lurched forward in outrage. Kingfisher quick, Seth nabbed the glass as, too late, Lex sharply commanded the barman to take it away.

Like a naughty kid, Seth took a big swig.

"You can't muck around with a bloke's knock-off drink," he told the Ox.

The big fella glowered. Seth knocked off another third of his drink.

"Okay, finish that and piss off," growled Lex.

Seth took his time. Then with his dignity intact, he went out towards the stairs. Passing open windows, he looked down to the car park and saw a fella smoking by a car. It was the grub from the Windsor Room – Mr. Spits.

Seth moved away from the window and thought of that tired chick getting home and finding the filth on her dress and feeling angry and hurt all over again. Just like the rotten bastard wanted.

Four merry fellas came out of the door and made for the exit. Quickly slotting in behind them, Seth went down the stairs. Outside, he kept them as cover until he could duck into the shadows. He watched the boys go to a car, then, keeping his head down, he moved along behind a row of vehicles.

He was a beast hunting, and the night's tribulations left his mind. He was in the here and now, and it was all that mattered. He'd hunted animals and caught big fish, but there was nothing quite like stalking a bloke.

Headlights came on, and he froze, waiting until the four laughing lads drove off. Then he drifted closer. When he got to a car's length away, the bastard's smoke foul on the still air, he paused and took a good look around.

There were no interior car lights, heads above roofs, or voices; no one at the stairs or downstairs entrance. He silently came up behind his quarry.

"Hey, mate," he said. The grub turned, peering through cigarette smoke into the darkness.

Seth hooked in a big, solid right, felt the bastard's nose break and scrunch across his face, and by golly, it was the best thing that had happened all night.

The Antidote

This is what I needed, thought Seth, pulling back on the throttle and making the 40 HP Evinrude outboard engine sing. This was the antidote to all the bullshit. Sitting in his mate Johnny Pep's Starcraft, he skimmed across the water towards the green bulk of Hinchinbrook Island.

The last few days had put his billy on to boil, that's for sure. He rarely got fired from a job; he usually walked first, but that hadn't been the end of it.

On the Monday, Evan had come over around seven in the morning, in footy shorts and canvas shoes, his knees and shins looking like something from a butcher's chiller. Seth had offered him a cuppa, but he declined.

Rubbing his balding head and looking glum, Evan told him that the fella who had got Seth sacked was talking about pressing assault charges.

"The magistrate knows his mates will drop you in it. But there's also patrons who were outside who'll back him up in court. Two, maybe more."

It was a total beat-up, but Seth knew this prick had a rich daddy, and rich daddies had lawyers.

"Y'know, maybe if ya just pissed off for a bit, this might not even make it to court," said Evan.

Seth now saw this message was the point of the visit, and he had agreed that might be a good idea.

And then his brother, what a bastard, doing a complete turnaround on what he'd said was swear-to-God true. Seth should have punched him. Gutted by guilt, he'd just yelled and shook his fist in the arsehole's face.

As ever, Alex had laughed it off. "He'll be right. Rory's a big boy. Mate, you bailed him up in church! Too fuckin' good! That's the Kelly boys for ya, hey?"

Yeah, Cairns could stick itself up its own clacker.

He'd pulled the pin on it this morning, driving nearly two hundred kilometres south on the streak of bitumen bullshit they called the Bruce Highway. The road was in such constant disrepair that the wags said, 'In town you drive on the left of it, and out of town you drive on what's left of it.'

In Cardwell he'd pulled off the Bruce and got ice, beer, and groceries. At the boat ramp by the jetty, he let the boat into the water, then parked the truck and trailer in the gravel car park off the highway.

And now he was off to Hinchinbrook, like he always said he would. He'd go to the lost beach he'd seen as a kid, bay hopping, fishing, and camping on the beaches. He'd have a look around, hike a bit, and swim at the waterfalls. His mate Walter had planted a seed the other night; now he was going to harvest it.

He'd brought cooking gear, a swag, his fishing rod, and speargun. The Starcraft came with tarps, ropes, a water drum, kero lanterns, mossie coils, a first aid kit, and even a bottle of Pep's Uncle Spiros's grappa, overproof white lightning that laid big blokes out. It was for emergencies, really. Besides, he had rum and a bit of the marijuana he'd grown. The only thing missing was Pep.

Raring to go, his fisherman mate had bailed out at the last minute. A fishing job had come along, but Pep had insisted he take the boat. Seth could fill up the fuel tanks when he was done and return the boat to his caravan site at Half Moon Bay.

Seth could have looked a bit harder for a companion, a chick ideally, but everyone he knew was busy, with the girls put off at roughing it on a jungle island. Truth was, he didn't really mind going by himself.

Looking forward to clearing his head, he wanted to go with whatever whim felt right. He'd be damn happy doing that for a while. And while he moseyed about the island, he could give some thought to future plans.

Sitting on the wood bench seat, he looked through the Plexiglas windscreen at the green water of the channel rushing past. Rising up into the sky ahead of him was the western range of Hinchinbrook Island, the peaks of Mt. Pitt and Barra Castle Hill catching tufts of cloud. To the north was the great curve of Rockingham Bay, dotted with the Family Islands, the outline of Bedarra lost against the dark mass of Dunk.

Passing Hecate Point, an anchorage a hundred metres off the big mangrove swamps of the island, he saw a bloke in a small cabin cruiser sitting on the back deck with a couple of rods out. They exchanged waves. It always paid to be friendly. Especially out here.

Turning the two-toned steering wheel, he went east, following the north coast of the island. It looked hot and rocky there, without mangroves or forest. The expanse of Missionary Bay slowly came into view: five kilometres across, edged by mangroves, with the central range of the island above it. With binoculars, he examined the far side of the bay as he drove. From a perusal of the map he'd brought, a 1:10,000, he knew there were big creeks in there, all terminating behind the seven kilometre barrier-dune beach of Ramsey Bay: this narrow tombolo of sand all that separated Missionary Bay from the Coral Sea.

Looking out for logs or shallows, he turned into the bay. When he was roughly in the middle, he killed the engine and used the binoculars to look for creek mouths. Pep said the second-last creek went almost to Ramsay Bay, and after a couple of hundred metres of bush-bashing, you'd come out onto the beach.

Firing up the Evinrude, he went further into the bay and soon saw the bottom: sand, mud, and clumps of seagrass passing by. Ten minutes later he slowed, used the glasses again, and saw the creek mouths: big, shadowed openings against the long sweep of green.

But going kilometres up a creek to then crash through mangrove swamp onto a hot beach wasn't sharpening his pencil, and he headed for the nearest creek instead.

Entering it, he dropped the speed to a few knots. The channel was pretty wide, keeping its breadth, and staying almost straight for a long way in. The mangrove thickets were metres high on either side, and above the thick green canopy, the range and mountain peaks glowed in the sun.

Cruising along, he saw some mudskippers lining a bit of exposed mud, the wake of the boat making them dive into the green water. When the creek narrowed, he turned off the engine, and as the boat slowed and came to a stop, he squirted on some Aerogard insecticide. The chemical smell was a bit rough, but the stuff worked.

Nevertheless, insects soon buzzed around, not biting, but real stoked he was there. Looking about, he listened to the plop and bubble of unseen creatures. There must be a million of them around him in this bay, every square metre teeming with fish, shells, worms, crabs, stingrays, and turtles, and all those microscopic wrigglers, and – in the creek something was chasing something.

The surface erupted as two small fish jumped for their lives. Water roiled behind them as their attacker flashed up into view – a strange monster's face on a small shark's body, the head like a hammerhead but curved back in a bonnet shape. With a whistle of appreciation, he watched it disappear. Mother Nature never failed to surprise.

If he could get paid to watch animals, he'd sign right up, even put on a government shirt. Maybe he could get a contract to count birds or something. But they'd probably issue him with a brush hook and over-boots and send him out to slog in some shithole in the sun. There was a National Parks office in Cardwell because Hinchinbrook had been a national park since the early thirties.

They'd done the right thing back then, but nowadays Queensland's religious peanut of a premier wanted to put oil rigs on the Great Barrier Reef. Luckily there was a Royal Commission into it, with Gough and the Feds going all out to stop it. That's why we vote Labor, Dad said.

For a horrible moment he imagined how a big oil spill would go here. It would be catastrophic, an evil blackness snuffing out all life, killing a world. He flashed on himself firing a big machine gun from a racing speedboat at an oil rig, sparks flying as bullets hit metal. This must be how revolutions start, he thought.

"Mass uprising of the people," he said to the mangroves. It was a term he'd heard on the radio and TV in the last few years, and he liked it. Filled with action, it sounded fair, with everybody pitching in and presumably getting an equal share. And you were sticking it to the man, which he didn't mind at all.

A shadow flashed over the creek. Looking up, he caught the shape of a fishing eagle, and he mouthed an oath. The bird was enormous! Blowing insects away from his face, he watched the sky between the glossy green leaves of the swamp, but the magnificent raptor didn't return.

For a laugh, he got out his rod, baited the hook, and chucked it in. Within ten seconds he got a bite, something small and lively. Getting it to the side, he saw a baby hammerhead jigging about, its creepy eyes out on stalks and its mouth full of tiny razors, and he cut the line.

Bloody hell, he thought, watching the shark vanish into the green water. The mangroves must be full of them. You wouldn't want to be incapacitated and bleeding in the water. The little buggers would give you a nipping you wouldn't forget, maybe even take you apart, bit by bit.

He spat over the side. He'd have a proper fish on the ocean side when he made camp there this afternoon. He put the rod away and drank some water.

Sunlight now beamed off the Perspex windscreen, and he saw that the prow of the boat was turning to one side. The tide was going out, pencil-thin mangrove seeds and tiny red, yellow, and green leaves moving on the surface. The Starcraft was moving downstream, and he could hear water running through the mangrove roots and the wet crackle and pop of newly exposed mud. He looked back, saw the creek getting shallower. Starting the engine, he turned about and began puttering back down the creek to the bay, a cloud of insects trying to keep up.

The boat bumped across the bottom, the prop catching for a second. It went forward, then bumped again, a wake like chocolate milkshake pluming out behind. He turned the wheel from side to side, the engine yowling, and made it through. He cautiously gave the engine more gas, and as he came out into the widest part of the creek, he saw mud banks glistening as rivulets of water ran through the hoops of mangrove roots.

The creek was draining quickly. He pushed the throttle up. Coming out into the bay, he saw channels and mud flats now exposed by the receding tide. With a thump, the boat hit the bottom and bounced off. It looked like the whole bloody bay was turning to mud! If he didn't get a wriggle on, he'd get caught out here. Then he'd have to spend hours in the baking sun while insects drank his sweat, and the ice in his Esky icebox melted fast.

When he got out into the deeper water of a channel, he went flat out for five minutes. Then, dropping speed, he looked back and saw the mud banks emerging around the creek mouths and the first herons coming in to land.

Relieved, he turned north and drove into the middle of the bay. It wasn't yet noon, but damn it, after all that he was going to have a beer. He slowed to a stop, opened the esky, and popped the crown of an ice-cold NQ Lager with the opener chained to the icebox.

The first swig was powerfully good, the next one right up there. With a sigh of satisfaction, he set the bottle on the bench seat and fired up the Evinrude again. With one hand on the throttle, he drove towards the wide mouth of the bay.

Dead ahead, he could see some of the Family Islands: Dunk, Bedarra, and Orpheus, where artists and writers still lived, and where they'd made a film starring James Mason and that young Pommy chick – blonde, smart-mouthed, and as curvy as hell.

He'd seen it at the Coral Drive-In with his brother and his mates. He just wanted to watch the movie, but they'd been idiots, shouting and whistling at the screen until they got chucked out. Seth had bailed from the car when they first started up, and he watched the rest of the movie leaning against the side of a truck.

Transfixed by the near-nude goddess swimming across the starry drive-in sky, he'd thought she was just about perfect. Mesmerizingly real, not like a Hollywood star, she played a sexy wildcat who lived on an island and caught crayfish. He was still in love with her.

Water skimmed past the Starcraft, and right in front of the boat – a pale, human-shaped body flashed towards him! With a bang of shock, he swerved hard, the boat up-siding, his beer flying in a spray of foam, things banging under the tarp, but – thank Christ – nothing thumping off the hull or shuddering through the prop.

He slowed right down and looked around. The animal was gone. You bloody idiot, he thought. You should have been awake to that – a dugong, just eating a bit of tucker in its own backyard. Ripping into the big mammal would have been a terrible thing to do.

He killed the engine, and the boat hissed through the water, seagrass and long banks of sand passing by. Then he saw a dugong feeding on seagrass. Silently passing the animal, the moving shadow of the boat nowhere near it, he watched the big, fat thing getting stuck into its meal.

The boat slowed and came to a stop, the seagrass like gardens around it. In the clear, shallow water he saw one of those odd bonnet-headed sharks again, the sunlight on the water throwing reflections on it, and what the hell? – the sawn-off little bugger was eating seagrass like a dugong, just chomping into it! He had to laugh out loud. How was this place? It even had hippy sharks.

Sitting back, with a light wind cooling his face, he took in the giant view. It was comic book stuff, the setting for a movie. It was a fantastic lost world, all right.

He finished the beer left in the bottle, decided against opening another, and headed east out of the bay towards Macushla Point. Two boats were moored there, people sitting on the back deck of one, and past the anchorage he went north to Cape Richards, right at the tip of the island.

Pep had told him that a resort called Nature Lovers had opened there earlier this year, and as he got closer to the rocky dome of the cape, he saw two yachts anchored in the lee of it, then a shed and a jetty by the shore. Though curious, he didn't want to stop in at the resort. He'd come for the remoteness of the island. Maybe another time.

Motoring by, he saw in the light forest by the water a prefab two-storey building that looked like staff quarters. The yachts' dinghies were on a tiny beach next to the jetty. With fishing all around and a bar and pool close by, it wasn't a bad spot to drop anchor for a spell.

There was a wooden pontoon jetty attached to a rock and concrete pier, a tin work shed, and two aluminium runabouts moored at the jetty, but no sign of the resort.

Moving past the granite cliffs of the cape, the sea looked different ahead. As he entered Rockingham Bay, he hit the swell and began thumping through the waves, bursts of spray hitting the windscreen. The sea ran rough out here, nothing like the calm expanse of Missionary Bay.

Tucked in past the cape was a small bay, with another headland at its end. It looked like the resort's beach, and keeping a few hundred metres offshore, he drove past it. Aside from a glimpse of a house by the headland and two kayaks on the beach, Nature Lover's was invisible.

The second headland of Cape Richards was smaller, its granite ledges, columns, and cliffs looking a million years in the making. The sculpted granite bluffs, three or four stories high, were stacked with grey boulders. Weathered smooth, a shed-sized rock seemed to have the serene face of an Asian god: the big, fat, cross-legged one.

As he drove around the point, he saw something move in the sunlight. On one of the granite towers there was a figure in shorts and t-shirt, sun-tanned and short-haired. He kept up speed, peering through the spray as the figure climbed a boulder and stood against the sky.

Something about the shape and stance made him slow down. He got the binoculars, stood with his left hand on the wheel, focused in, and saw bare legs, the curve of hips, and a cap of blonde hair. It was a chick up there, standing as still as a statue of a goddess.

And how was this? She also had binoculars, and she was looking right back! Taking his eyes from the glasses, he laughed in disbelief. Spread-legged on the bench seat, he felt a thrill of excitement go through him.

He used the glasses again. The Starcraft bucked, skating the waves. Spume flew as he tried to keep her in view. She'd be a guest from the resort, probably with a bloke in tow. But when he gave her a wave, she waved back, and his grin slid out of control.

He looked hard at the shoreline and saw cliffs, rocks, more rocks, but nowhere to land. When he looked back up at the cape, she was gone. The goddess had hopped down off her pedestal.

A strip of bright sand appeared on the shore, a blur of salt mist above it. But it was beyond the cape, and he now saw it was the foreshortened view of a beach ahead that was a kilometre or more long. The cape became forested, and he soon saw the start of the beach. The resort couldn't be that far from it by foot, half an hour at best.

Some proper breakers were coming into the beach, and he timed his landing between waves. Cutting the motor, he went to the transom and raised it. As the hull touched sand, he jumped into the waves with the mooring rope and swiftly pulled the rolling boat up onto the sand.

He knew from the map that this was the northern part of Shepard Bay. Looking around, he saw an eagle soaring hundreds of metres up. As he watched, the bird swooped down, folded its wings, and fell like a stone into the sea, re-emerging seconds later with a fish in its claws.

A grin split Seth's face; his scalp tingled with atavistic joy. Witnessing this animal at work eking out a few more days of survival was inspiring. I'm so bloody complicated compared to it, he thought. Too much thinking, too much mucking about, too much stuff to carry around. Animals had it over humans every time.

Grateful for his sunnies, he watched the tinsel glitter of the sea, looking for the splash of a fish, maybe the head of a turtle, even the fin of a dolphin. If he lost the sunglasses, he'd improvise, using a strip of coconut fibre with a slit to peer from. Henry, his mate from Torres Strait, had shown him how to do this, and it worked well.

He walked to where the beach began, the green forest throwing shade over drifts of pumice stone. There was a spray of golden orchids growing on an old dead tree, and, no surprise there, a track that must go to the resort. He pondered it, then decided to stay on the beach. He'd have a fish. See what happened. And stay the night.

He got his rod, then put a little tackle box, some bait, and his canteen into his canvas bag. Hanging the glasses around his neck, he slung the bag over his shoulder and headed to the rocks at the start of the headland.

As he walked along the waterline, he watched as a wave receded and saw scores of *pipis* now exposed, standing up in the sand. He scooped up some of the little shellfish before they could burrow back in. They were perfect bait.

Coming off the foam-washed sand, he hopped across the warm rocks. Not far from the sand was a big, old beach almond, its mass of thick, gnarly branches making wide, cool bars of shade above the rocks. Sliding the rod up onto a big lower limb, he climbed up onto it, then put the rod up onto another branch: a fat slab of rough, tiled bark that hung out over the water.

Up there he found a place to sit. Snapping off a small branch, he hung the bag from the hook he'd made. With the rod's handle trapped safely under his thigh, he took a leisurely look around.

It was a good spot – an eye on the world. He could look up the length of the beach and also see anyone coming out of the track onto the sand. And right beneath him through the clear blue water was the bottom, littered with dark rocks and chunks of dead coral.

Straight up, he saw fish, and he baited up with a pipi. As he readied to cast, he saw they'd gone. He watched, saw no more movement, but no matter. It was nice and shady, with a good breeze. He was on island time now, and there were plenty of fish in the sea.

In an unhurried rhythm he cast out and reeled in, again and again and again. Through the rod and the line, he felt the roll of the sea, and in a blissful torpor, his thoughts flew out over the horizon and across the Coral Sea.

It was the most amazing thing: that the Trobriands, the Solomons, New Hebrides, New Caledonia, and Fiji were over there, all so much closer than England or America. But he had no real idea what they were like. Like coming to Hinchinbrook, he'd have to go and see one day.

Shadows filled the spaces in the rocks, creeping out like the tide from the tree line. The beach had lost all sun, the sea now a dark steely blue, and its gurgling, plopping, and lapping, unceasing and never-repeating, was hypnotic.

He stopped casting and gazed anew at the horizon, and a feeling came over him that turned his mind upside down. He was sitting just a tad out over the water, but right there were the rocks of the shoreline that formed the natural boundary of the human realm. It's where we crawled up onto, he thought. It's where we don't drown, where we live and breathe.

But right now, he felt that he was on the *other* side of

this edge and that the main event was actually out there in the big blue. That was the real world, boundless and free. Uncluttered by thought or design, the ocean and the sky made a continent unto themselves, a place bigger and deeper than anywhere on the crowded, cluttered earth. It was the strangest bloody feeling, and he liked it.

Coming out of his oceanic daydream, he sighed and cast out again. Nothing was biting, but he didn't mind. There was steak in the esky and days of fishing to come.

Reeling in his line, he saw with sudden disbelief – a pair of huge eyes just beneath the surface. Big and round, half a metre between them, the pupils were infallible slits. A wave had just expended against the rocks below him, and the sea monster suspended there was looking right up at him. He felt a spurt of visceral fear – pure monkey instinct at being bailed up by a big predator.

Then the sea fell back, and the eyes moved apart, one moving quicker than the other, and Seth saw the long pale bodies of two big squid. For a second they had lined up perfectly, their eyes making the illusion of a giant face.

Mightily relieved, he laughed, too bloody loudly, but so what? There was no bastard around to hear.

He cast aimlessly now, the day fading. With no clouds around, his swag on the sand would do for tonight. Just as he decided to chuck it in, he caught a fish: a kilo-sized bream, and like the happy ape he was, he climbed down out of his tree and killed it.

While drinking two beers, he made a fire and fried the fish with sweet potato and broccoli, and it was real nice. After cleaning up, he had a nip of Uncle Spiro's grappa to remind him of what Saturn V rockets ran on, and, Jesus, it was strong. You wouldn't want to drink it by the fire, or anywhere near a naked flame for that matter.

It was time for a normal drink, and he made himself a Bundy and cola – on ice. Out here on the edge of the Coral Sea, it was pure bloody luxury. Grinning, he took a good slug of it, then rolled a joint and fired it up with his Zippo. As the light faded, he took a quick look at the map, then leisurely thought about what had happened so far this year and what he might do next.

He'd just grown a good whack of marijuana with his mate Robbie and two of his mates – good blokes he'd connected with. It was the second time he'd done this with Robbie, the first time just the two of them. But bigger was better, with the yield from this crop coming in at over a hundred pounds. It was a bit of work living out in the scrub, but it was a hell of a lot better than picking tobacco, chasing prawns, or sitting in a stuffy office.

Careful as a crow in these matters, Robbie was looking for suitable buyers, something Seth was happy for him to do. He had the contacts, and his mad mate Simon was happy to ride shotgun on any deal. Yeah, woe betide any bastard stupid enough to muck around with those boys.

Flicking the roach away, Seth felt pretty bloody good about things. Growing dope was a top way to make a buck. When he got his share, he'd bank a third, paying tax on it as fishing and other work, keep a couple of grand, and hide the rest in waterproof packs of the new fifties.

Working as a bouncer in Cairns had kept him ticking along the last few months, but soon he'd be set for a while: a free bird. He could go to Darwin like he'd been thinking, and if he didn't like it there, he could catch a jet to Sydney.

Or Perth. And if he got a passport, he could go overseas.

It was fully dark now, the stars a silent city overhead. He rolled out his swag and lay back. With the waves on the beach like a thousand sighing voices, he smiled at his good fortune and drifted into sleep.

Better Than the Movie

Light filled the world. Seth opened his eyes and grunted agreeably at the sea and sky. He could smell the salt in the air and feel the grit of sand in his teeth. This was beach bumdom, and it was grand.

As he made breakfast, he saw that there were now two fishing eagles working the beach, their white bodies and heads catching the sun. Large adults, no doubt paired for life, they flew off towards a range of hills at the far end of the beach each time they caught something.

The next time this happened, he got out the glasses and watched an eagle disappear into the forested headland. After cleaning up, he drove down the other end of the bay.

It was a good deal calmer there, the water clear and shallow. Puttering in, he looked for fish, saw bugger all, and after dropping anchor, got his hat and canteen and walked to where the sand turned into a jumble of granite boulders, the spherical rocks almost purple in colour.

He leant against a boulder and waited. Soon enough, an eagle came flying above the beach, a fish in its claws. Its shadow sped along the sand, then flashed over the rocks a few metres from where he stood. Turning from the hot granite, he raised the glasses and saw the eagle fly to the point of the headland and vanish into a stand of trees. There'd be a nest there, complete with a couple of chicks screeching for a feed.

Climbing up for a closer look sort of appealed, but it was too far and too hot. Another time, with a mate with a good camera. They could go the full National Geographic.

He watched the water. Still no fish. Heat radiated off boulders. There were no shady trees here, so he went back to the other end and pulled the boat up the sand. He got out his little speargun, the diving knife, and a net bag on a rope for his catch. He'd trail the bag a metre behind him, as a shark-ripped artery here would mean certain death; his last minutes a red mist of pain as sharks fought over who was going to eat more of him.

At the tree line, movement caught his eye. Two people were coming out of the track he'd seen yesterday: a barrel-shaped bloke with skinny white legs and, nice, the short-haired blondie he'd seen up on the rocks yesterday. Yeah, it was good he'd stuck around. Leaving the gear on the gunwale, he sauntered up to the bow.

Blondie and the bloke both had water canteens, and neither looked happy. As they silently came towards him, Seth could tell that they weren't together or even friends. With faces like that, they were probably family.

The bloke, late forties, sun-spotted and balding, was sweaty, red-faced, and unshaven. Shorter than Seth by a few inches, his shins were scarred, and his waist carried decades of grog. He had the look of a desk jockey long ago promoted from a world of hard yakka.

They stopped at the boat, and the man put his canteen down and took out a pack of smokes. Blondie nodded in greeting. She looked a few years younger than him, stocky but nowhere near chubby: definitely an outdoors girl. In canvas shoes, shorts over a swimsuit, she wasn't sweating.

The bloke said nothing as he busied himself lighting up. His eyes went over the boat but didn't make it to Seth.

"G'day," said Seth to Blondie. The bloke grunted and squinted up the beach.

"I'm Cath," said the girl. "I work at the resort back there at Cape Richards."

"Oh, that's great," said Seth, failing to hold back a grin. She smiled back, and he felt a wave of pleasure. The bloke watched them now, looking almost jealous. Too bad, dad, thought Seth. You're old, and you look like shit.

"I'm Seth," he said to Cath.

"Seth? Jesus," said the bloke, his scalp running with perspiration.

Seth kept smiling. His name was biblical, chosen by his university-educated father. Blokes had stirred him about it for years, but he didn't give a rat's arse. And it sorted out the dickheads from the get-go.

Hawking phlegm onto the sand, the bloke showed Seth yellow teeth, then looked at Cath's legs and chest like she was a yearling at a stockyard sale. A grunt of inquiry included Seth in the inspection. Whatcha think of them apples? it said. Seth blinked. She did look real nice, but this was bloody rude.

Still openly looking, the old bastard made a filthy little sound, then luxuriously blew out smoke.

"You right there, mate?" said Seth.

The bloke turned to him. "Whatcha say?"

"What, you never seen a woman before?" said Seth.

"You cheeky bastard." Flicking his cigarette away, the bloke stepped forward, a fug of grog sweat rising off him.

Seth also stepped forward. Looking down at the wet red

face, he wanted to put his fist into it. Instead, he stared an unblinking message into the man's eyes. After a few face-saving seconds, the bastard stepped back.

"Ahh, get fucked you, young prick," he said. He turned and strode off up the beach.

"You're welcome to her," he yelled over his shoulder.

Seth watched him go with real hate. Turning to Cath, he was cheered to see a good smile on her face. They both laughed, and the tension blew away in the breeze.

"You're the fella I saw yesterday," she said.

Seth made a little bow. "The very same."

"Well, thanks for sticking up for me." She nodded at the figure going up the beach. "He's a bastard."

She pulled out a pack of Rothmans and lit one up. Seth felt a stab of dismay, but he'd wear it for the cause. And besides, pashing wasn't everything that chicks did.

Cath blew out smoke. She looked browned off.

"He came onto me as we walked over here, hey."

"The dirty dog," said Seth. "Lay his paws on you?"

"Almost. I was getting a bit worried. If he'd kept it up, I would have raced back to the resort."

"He's a guest?"

"Yeah. Last night he was with a couple from Townsville. I was waitressing, and they got proper tanked over dinner, and 'cause I have today off, I said I'd bring them here. But the couple were too hungover this morning, so I ended up with Mr. Pig."

"Ah, don't worry about that idiot," said Seth.

They smiled at each other again. Cath smoked, casually taking in his chest and arms. He didn't mind. Chicks liked a gander as much as blokes did.

"You going spear-fishing, then?" Cath eyed his gear.

"Yeah, just along the rocks here. Not too far."

"I'll come too."

She wasn't asking. He liked that.

"Yeah, if ya want."

The boom-boody-boom went off in his chest as she took her shoes and shorts off. He had to snatch his eyes away and find the spare mask and snorkel. Looking real nice in a blue swimsuit, Cath waded in on strong legs, then swam beneath the waves to get away from the beach.

Seth followed, watching her: all curvy blue and golden brown. She swam smart, keeping a level distance from the rocks, awake to the gravity and mass of moving water and where it could put you.

Her bum glowed in the sunlight, and he felt like a perv looking at it, so he caught up and swam side by side with her. Not far from the tree where he'd fished yesterday, he gestured for her to stop, and they bobbed about, kicking and paddling to stay in place.

They checked out the water around them, Seth looking for those squid. Small fish flickered like animated leaves over rocks, and down where the granite tumbled onto the sandy sea floor, larger fish moved.

Settling the rubber mouthpiece between his teeth, Seth cocked the speargun, then swam down into a sandy gutter between the rocks. He cruised along, his bulk against the light sending small fish flying.

A few metres down, he saw a dark shape of the right size loitering behind a rock. He swam in fast, aimed, and fired. The spear went into the seabed in a puff of sand, and the fish swam off.

Feeling silly, he retrieved the spear. At the surface he reloaded it. Cath swam in close, her smile bright, her voice sure. "Let me have a go."

"You reckon you'll get one, hey?" said Seth.

"I have before," she said. "With Dad and my brothers."

He passed her the cocked speargun, digging the grin of pleasure as she took it. Holding the little speargun above the chop, she looked it over. "No line?"

"Yeah, so nothing real big. A few kilos, max. It's like a kid's speargun. Good for a quick meal."

Water danced between them. A wave hit her shoulders and broke over her neck in a silvery spray.

"Aim for the head," he said. "You get a hit, and I'll swim in and grab hold of it."

She probably wouldn't get a proper headshot, and he'd have to race after the fish, but what the hell.

Satisfied, she dived under. Hot with appreciation, Seth followed. Propelled forward with strong strokes of her legs, Cath looked for a target. They passed over fallen granite, and in a mound of rocks, something flickered in the light. She angled in off the sun, hiding in its glare. She raised the speargun, held it out, began to aim.

A bubble of glee burst from Seth's mouthpiece – the synchronicity was mind-blowing. Cath was even blonde. This was like that movie on Dunk Island!

She quickly swam down, the speargun an extension of her outstretched arm. Closing in, spearhead steady, she shot the fish.

With a burst of speed, he swam in, grabbed the spear, feeling a single wiggle from the fish before it went still. Surfacing, he held the spear up and saw that the fish was dead, the shaft right through its brain. He looked around and saw Cath right there.

"Good shot," he said.

"Yeah," she said matter-of-factly, like what else did he expect? The self-assurance was real sexy.

"You hungry?" he said.

"Yeah, I am."

"Let's go cook it, then."

She grinned, and water splashed off her teeth.

They swam back and walked side-by-side to the boat.

"You want a towel?" said Seth, sneaking a casual look.

"In this sun? Nah, I'll dry off soon enough."

Seth put the fish, a nice little snapper, on the back transom. He'd slice the fillets off, give the head and frame back to the ocean, and then –

"What an idiot," said Cath. "He left his water behind."

Seth turned and saw the forgotten canteen on the sand in the shadow of the hull. They looked up the salt-misted beach, and Cath sighed unhappily.

"I'm responsible for him, and he drank a lot last night."

Seth got the glasses and began scanning the beach. Three quarters of the way along, he saw a figure. Problem was, it was horizontal. While they'd been swimming in the cool blue sea, the idiot had collapsed.

"What a numbskull," said Seth. "He's down."

It didn't take long to get to him, the Evinrude going flat out. He was unconscious; spittle dried around his mouth, his face beef-red, the sweating stopped. They tried to get some water down his mouth, then put a wet towel around his head and armpits. Seth slapped his cheeks but got no response.

"Let's get him in the boat," said Seth.

"Bloody hell!" wailed Cath.

He brought the Starcraft in, and they lifted him onto the gunwale. He was heavy, his white gut flopping from his shirt, and while Cath held him there, Seth got into the boat. They pulled him onto the bench seat, his skinny legs splaying out into the space at the bow. Pep had installed duckboards there, and the bloke's shoes squeaked off the wet timber.

As Cath held the boat, Seth pushed him up against the gunwale and let go, but he slid down, his head dropping towards the bench seat. Catching him, Seth pushed him back, then watched him start to slide again.

He slammed his hand in and held it there. He looked at Cath in commiseration. It was going to be a real bunfight for her to hold him up as they raced back to the resort.

"This fat bastard is going to end up sliding down there. Probably break an ankle or a leg," he began.

"I'll drive us back," said Cath. "You can hold him up."

"Yeah? You can do that?"

"I've driven boats. Some bigger than this," she said.

"With your dad and brothers, right?"

"Yep." She stared at him.

"Okay, sure. Go for it."

It was a bit of a dance, but she got the Starcraft's nose out. She was light-footed, smooth biceps flexing, and she looked real nice hopping onboard and slotting in behind the wheel. Firing up the Evinrude, she drove out into the bay, goosing the power the further out they went. Okay, thought Seth, she's got a handle on this.

He could feel her warm thigh pressed against his leg,

the curve of her hip against his. Then he smelt sweated-out grog, and he had to laugh. Bloody hell, it had gone from heaven to hell in fifteen minutes: spearfishing with a real beaut of a girl one minute, then cuddling up to this stinking bastard the next.

Around the headland, she reduced speed and tacked to avoid the swell, the boat jumping along the sets of waves. As soon as she got past the cape and into the bay, she went at full speed towards the resort end. Seth gave her an approving look, but she was too focused to notice.

At the beach, she dropped anchor, and they levered the idiot out. With his arms over their shoulders, they got him across the sand and onto a track in the forest.

As they began staggering along it, a voice called out.

"Hey, Cath. What's going on?" There was a bloke on the track ahead and a woman behind him. With a clink of bottles, he put down a bag and hurried forward.

"Oh, Rowie! It's the guest in number three, Rob Mara. Didn't drink enough water, and he's collapsed," said Cath. "Oh God, I served him so many drinks last night."

"Right," said the woman, and she turned and ran back up the track. The bloke came in, and as he took the weight from Cath, he nodded at Seth.

"Rowie?" said Seth.

"Yep, that's me. Look, we'll take him up the back to the dining room verandah. We'll keep it nice and quiet, hey."

Rowie looked mid-forties, wiry, and strong. They lifted the bastard's feet off the ground and hurried him up the path. They came into the resort area, gardens everywhere, and passed a white prefab building. A fella in cook's gear stood staring at them from the doorway.

In the cool gloom of the restaurant, the blue flicker of a pool behind the railing, Seth and Rowie laid their burden down on the polished wood floor. Seth stood back, looked around. Wicker cutlery boxes sat on a timber sideboard, and linen-covered tables were set with silverware and cut-glass vases filled with hibiscus and croton.

Staff descended on the limp guest, setting up a fan and laying on wet towels. Seth moved back, ice clinked, and Cath started answering questions. Rowie was talking to the woman from the track, her hand on his arm like she was his missus. Seth quietly went down the stairs and took the track back to the beach. He needed a beer.

The bottles in the esky were still nice and cold. He took his shirt off and splashed some ice water from the esky over his chest. He cracked a beer, and it went down quick. He considered another, but Cath was in the picture now.

He checked out both headlands with the glasses and then the Brook Islands a few kilometres out. He looked up the beach. It sure was a nice spot for a resort.

After a bit, Rowie appeared on the beach, his bag slung from his shoulder. He came over, sinewy and bronzed by a life in the sun, a little bluebird tattoo peeking out from beneath his open shirt.

"You're Seth?" The older man looked like he wanted to be sure about it. Seth nodded, and they shook hands.

"So you and your missus got the day off?" said Seth.

"Nah, we did the morning shift. Knocked off now. Was about to have a beer with Margie, and you lot turned up."

"You wanna beer, Rowie?"

"Mate, let's go down the beach. Staff ain't encouraged to drink up this end. The guests an' all."

"Yeah, no worries." Seth gestured at the boat. "Hop in."

At the end of the beach in the lee of the headland, Seth brought the boat in and chucked in the anchor. They got out, and the older man took two cans of Foster's out of his bag, handed one to Seth, and then lit a cigarette.

"Mate, thanks. Lucky you were there. Cath's got a good head on her shoulders, but she couldn't have got him back on her own. There were supposed to be four of them going to North Ramsey, but it didn't turn out that way."

"No worries," said Seth. "Cath was more than great. She drove the boat because the bloke couldn't sit up."

Rowie laughed. "Good for her."

"So how's the bloke doing?"

"He should be right in a few hours. Bloody idiot."

Seth chuckled softly. Rowie looked over his cigarette at him, his amiable, slightly distracted eyes now flint sharp.

"So Mara just walked off on his own?" he said.

"Ah yeah, he seemed a bit . . . y'know –"

"Of a bastard?"

Seth laughed. Rowie nodded in affirmation.

"Yeah, he got real drunk last night. Shot his mouth off. Didn't want to leave when the bar closed. And a bit bloody rude too. No guest has got the right to act like that."

Seth looked at the sea. Rowie smoked, watching him. "You see any of that?" he said.

Seth looked at him and nodded. "Yep."

Rowie grunted wryly. "You didn't like it?"

Seth shook his head. "No, I didn't."

"Rude to Cath, was he?"

Seth nodded. Rowie frowned.

"So, you fronted him?"

"Yeah, I did."

"And he didn't like it and walked off like a little girl?"

"Like a little girl."

The two men laughed, and Rowie saluted Seth with his beer. "Doubly glad you were there, then," he said.

They finished their beers, and Seth said, "My shout."

He got two NQs out of the esky, and they went up and sat in the soft sand by the trees. With a little prompting, Rowie told Seth all about the island's ocean side: the beaches, creeks, and waterfalls, and the old track that linked most of the bays on the east coast. National Parks, bushwalkers, and the army used it infrequently, and in some places it wasn't easy to see.

"Basically follows the lay of the land," said Rowie. "Use your common sense and you'll pick it up again."

When Seth mentioned the possibility of buying fuel from the resort in a few days' time, Rowie said he'd have a word with Ted, the resort's mechanic and handyman.

Now they heard voices calling from up the beach. It was Cath and Rowie's missus, Margie. As they came up, they pretended to whinge about not getting a ride on the boat.

Margie looked older than Rowie, but she wasn't tanned like him. Cath winked at Seth, their little rescue adventure now a bond between them. She sat in a flash of legs across from Seth, and Margie sat next to Rowie. With a big sigh, she stretched out her legs.

"Dearie me. Turning mattresses, in this heat, and all the laundry too," she said. "Give us a beer, sweetie."

"Would you like one of mine?" said Seth. He hopped up and took a few paces towards the boat.

"Yes, please," said Cath. Seth gave her a look of mock

admonishment for butting in, and she smirked at him.

"What are you drinking?" said Margie.

"NQ Lager. It's cold."

"Sounds lovely. They have it at the bar."

"Oh, I love NQ," said Cath. Margie gave her a bemused smile and lit a cigarette.

Seth got the beers, then got the full interrogation from Margie, Cath listening and grinning like she already knew it all. Margie was cheery but thorough. With quick replies and a couple of lies, he got through work, marital status, and family pretty quick, though he yielded up a few things that he'd never have told a bloke. Women were good at doing that.

Then Margie told him about the seaplane crashing into the sea on opening day – it was lucky no one got seriously hurt – and Cath told him about the huge goannas at the resort and how the lizards tried to get into the restaurant when nobody was around. She and the chef would have to chase them off with brooms.

She was pretty funny telling it, completely animated with lots of arms and hands, her mouth working and eyes lit. Sipping his beer, Seth lapped her up.

Then a weird screaming started up in the bush behind them, a high-pitched, cartoon sound like a cat on helium.

"What in God's name is that?" said Margie.

They all jumped up, a packet of smokes from someone's lap throwing cigarettes to the sand, and hurried to see.

"Oh no! It's getting eaten," said Cath.

In a she-oak, a big green tree frog was being swallowed whole. Wailing, its front legs flailing, it was caught in the mouth of a tree snake.

"Either of you going to save it?" said Margie.

Rowie and Seth shook their heads.

"Ah, it's nature, aye," said Seth, not wanting to deny the snake a feed.

"It's an awful racket. I'm going for a walk," said Margie.

"Same here," said Cath.

Beers in hand, they walked off down the beach. Seth watched Cath start talking to Margie. Then the screaming stopped, and he turned back. Mouth now closed, the tree snake hung there, the lump in its body ridiculous.

"It's a goner," said Rowie, and he sunk his beer.

They went and sat down and opened fresh beers. Rowie lit a smoke, and they watched the sea in an easy silence. Yeah, thought Seth, this is what island life is all about.

Rowie watched Cath and Margie up the beach, and after a bit he looked at Seth. "You're a good bloke aren't you?"

Knowing what this was about, Seth nodded. "Especially with sheilas."

"Yeah?" said Rowie, his eyes gone rock hard again.

"I like sheilas," said Seth. Putting his hands together in prayer, he smiled wistfully. "I *love* them."

Rowie smiled at that, then nodded slowly.

"Yep. Me and Margie been together fifteen years."

Seth waited for more, but there wasn't any.

Rowie puffed on his smoke, his eyes back on the two women. When they turned, laughing, and came walking back, he took a swig of his can and nodded.

"Cath listens to Margie," he said.

Seth drank beer, looked at the massive granite boulders of the headland: smooth, grey, and white, stacked up like ruins. She looked great standing up there yesterday.

"You're still here," said Cath as they came up.

"Yeah, the view's alright, aye," said Seth.

Cath's smile was more than promising, and he felt a zip of excitement. Thank you, Margie.

They talked a bit more, then Rowie said he was going to listen to the cricket on the radio. Margie said she'd go and get him some staff dinner.

"The tucker here's not too bad," she said.

"Lots of fish," said Rowie.

Margie looked at Cath. "You two behave yourselves."

"I'll keep an eye on her," said Seth.

Cath laughed. "Who made you head prefect?"

Rowie shook Seth's hand. "Big thanks again."

"No worries. All's good that ends well."

The trust in Rowie's eyes was no small thing.

"C'mon, love," said Margie, and they got up and set off up the shadowed beach.

"See you," said Cath, watching them go.

Seth saw a tiny scar on her inner thigh.

"They worry," she said, turning to him.

"That's fair enough."

"But you're a nice fella, right?"

"If it weren't so, you wouldn't be here."

Cath stared at him, then nodded. "Yeah, that's right. It's women's intuition. We do have it. We have to have it."

Seth thought about Mr. Pig unconscious on the beach at North Shepherd. He got two more beers, and they sat drinking in silence, their eyes on the sea.

When Rowie and Margie finally disappeared into the tree line by the resort, Cath moved across the sand on her bum and gave him a big kiss on the mouth. Then with a giggle, she upended her beer, finishing it, and jumped up. Looking down at him, she gave him a defiant smile that said, I'm drunk and I don't care.

Seth grinned at her, but he wasn't giving her another beer just yet. He'd seen too many girls go up fast, then splash down in a pool of spew.

"You want to go for a walk?" he said.

Spinning around on the spot, she flung out her arms like a dancer in a show. "Where to?"

Seth finished his beer and got up.

"Just along the beach?"

"Why not?"

They went down to the water, and Cath began skipping and kicking through the foaming semicircles. He picked up burny bean seeds, flat black ovals, and skimmed them out past the waves, Cath cheering each skip on the water.

As they got closer to the resort, they walked side-by-side. Cath casually took his hand in hers, and his heart skipped like a bloody burny bean.

"So where is everyone?" said Seth. "Shouldn't there be a beach bar and deck chairs?"

"At sunset some guests might come down with a drink and sit on the sand, but mostly they stick around the bar and restaurant. We have the run of the beach after dark."

"Must be fun working here," said Seth.

Cath gave him that mystery look that women seemed to have. It said a lot but gave away nothing. He was never sure what it meant or what they were thinking, but he'd never been game to ask.

"Yeah, it's pretty nice." Cath looked out at the horizon, the Brook Islands lit by the far sunlight in the west.

"You been over there?" said Seth, nodding at the trio of pink and gold islands. She shook her head. "I've been to Goold and Garden and over to Dunk one time."

"You wanna go?" he said.

She laughed. "What, like now?"

The sea looked okay past the headlands, and the rows of clouds to the north weren't moving closer.

"Yeah. Take twenty minutes. We could stay the night."

Cath looked at him, and he liked what he saw.

"Yeah, okay," she said. "But you have to bring me back early, though. I start at seven."

"Your wish is my command."

She slapped his arm. "I might just hold you to that."

"Do your worst."

The look she gave him made his stomach hollow out and his swinging bits hum.

"You got bedding?" said Cath, now all businesslike.

"Yeah, yeah, all of that."

"Fifteen minutes, okay? I'll just go tell them and grab some things."

"Take twenty."

She turned and ran up the beach, her laugh sending a squirt of excitement up him. As he went to get the boat, he grinned madly. This turn of events was turning out real sweet!

Sticking around North Shepard had been worth it. And he was glad he hadn't got heavy with Mr. Pig. It wouldn't have looked too good with him collapsing and all, and a second assault charge was the last thing Seth needed.

He brought the Starcraft up the beach, and it was closer to twenty-five minutes before Cath came out of the trees and ran down to him. She looked nice in a loose top, wow, no bra, and a pair of baggy shorts. Her hair looked damp, and she smelt of shampoo and baby powder. She had a bag, a towel, and a pillow, and Seth stowed them all under the tarp on the boat.

When he turned back, she was behind the wheel.

"Oh, be my guest," he said.

"Ta," she said, looking pleased as punch.

"So you're okay with reefs and stuff out there?"

"Yep. If I go due north past Goold, then turn east, I'll miss the shoals. There's no reef until real close to the islands, and I'll be going slow then."

Impressed, he pushed the boat out. Hoisting himself onboard, he slid onto the bench seat. She started up and pushed the throttle forward, and soon they were out of the bay, with the domes of the cape receding behind them. Above them, great cloud ships drifted, and when they passed through lines of leaves and driftwood, the swell began rolling in from the Coral Sea. This was where the ocean came around Hinchinbrook into Rockingham Bay.

It was too loud to talk, and Cath kept her eyes on the water ahead. He watched the water too, throwing her glances from time to time, and, man, she looked more than cool; her hair a golden shimmer, her strong, jaw set, and her bare feet braced on the hull. She caught his eye once and winked, and he felt truly glad to be alive.

Behind them, the island looked monolithic: a great big slab of forever, its spine of peaks black against the blue. The symmetrical bulk of Goold Island receded, and the islands of the Family Group began to fill Rockingham Bay.

Fish jumped ahead – a couple of mackerel looking like

they were running across the water, and a dolphin stuck its head out and caught one, the mackerel seemingly cut in two by the bite. Mouth open in surprise, Cath pointed at the splashes in the water.

Fifteen minutes later and the Brook Islands were right there: white sand, granite rocks, scrub, and low forested hills, with the sand cays between them golden in the light. They got closer, passing over reef, and Seth stood, looking for coral bommies that might hit the hull or prop. On the northernmost island, there was a line of sand sticking out a hundred metres, and Cath drove towards it.

The sandspit was a spearhead of pure white, with lines of little waves rippling along its edge. Surrounded by the bluest, clearest water, it looked like something from a glossy magazine: a Bacardi or Peter Stuyvesant ad.

Cutting the speed right down, Cath cruised into the lee of the spit. A dark shape moved in the water against the pale sand. Spooked by the boat, it darted out into the indigo deep. Cath killed the engine, and the boat swished onto the sand. They sat for a moment, digging the silence, then Seth hopped out and threw in the anchor.

"Well, you were pretty fast," he began, but Cath jumped out, let out a wild yell of laughter, and ran full tilt up along the spit.

Laughing too, he gave chase, and she whooped louder. He was out to catch her, and she knew it, but he let her get to the end, where they stopped in astonishment. Right out in the sea now, it was like they were standing on the water.

He put his arm around her, drew her in, and they stood side-by-side on the last bit of sand where the boundary between solid ground and sea melted away.

"Ohhhh," said Cathy softly. "This is magic."

"So are you," he said. She laughed and snuggled closer. He cupped her bottom with his hand. She gasped, waited, then giggled as she let him feel her up.

Then with a mad Indian whoop, she pulled away and pelted back down the sandspit. He gave chase, and when he caught up, they ran together, yelling and carrying on like kids at sports day.

Then he roared and grabbed her, and she screamed as he swung her up behind him. Piggybacking her to the boat, he felt her fingers in his hair, her smooth calves in his hands, and her breasts warm and soft against his back. When he put her down, she slapped his arse.

"You brute," she said happily. "You're a bloody pirate."

Smiling fit to burst, Seth got the rug, the cushions, and his swag and laid them on the sand. Cath was impressed. She put her bag and pillow on one side of the rug and sat down in the middle. Seth put the esky on the other side, then he sat and contemplated their next drink. Cath lit up a smoke, and he got up and sat upwind.

"Oh, I'm sorry," said Cath. "It's a terrible habit."

Seth shrugged like he didn't care.

"You smoke anything else?" he said.

"Like what – cigars?"

He waited as she took a drag. Then she frowned and blew out smoke in disgust.

"You don't mean mari-u-ana, do you? No way. I value my mind too much to muck about with that stuff. Have you seen those hippie sorts? You ever hear some of them speak? No wonder they call it dope."

Seth made a noise that could pass for agreement.

"Just a couple of puffs is all it takes," warned Cath. "I don't want to ruin my life. I might never come back."

"What about rum?" said Seth.

"You got some?"

"And coke and ice."

"Well, hello!"

He made them drinks, the glasses tinkling with chunks of ice. Sharing a grin, they clinked drinks, then took in an absolute pearler of a sunset.

It was the one millionaires wanted: the water a limpid metallic blue, the sky an open furnace, with banks of deep purple cloud capping the high ranges fifteen kilometres away on the mainland. This was a good spot to see it all.

"Well, Seth," said Cath after a while. "I have to say it's nice that you're not trying to jump all over me."

"I could, though," said Seth.

Her smile promised everything. She rummaged in her cloth bag. "Just so you know." She held up a small foil package, and Seth's heart, everything really, leapt.

"Just one?" he said.

Cath laughed and pointedly put the condom on the rug between them. Seth gave her a salute, and they finished their drinks, smirking at each other like two cats in a milking shed. This *is* fun, he thought, not going for it straight up and just stretching out feeling toey like this.

Then something pinched at him, a thought he should heed, and he hopped up and went around the other side of the boat. He got out the soap and a towel, and using fresh water from the drum, washed his pits and bits.

Cath gave him a round of applause, and he shot her a smarmy grin, like he was the good kid at school camp.

"Well, aren't you a nice boy," laughed Cath.

"Good things happen to nice boys," said Seth.

Cath pulled a face, waggled her head from side to side. He rinsed and towelled off, half hoping she might come around the boat and tease him while he was naked, but she just sat there sipping her drink, the mystery look on her face again.

After pulling on clean shorts, he crouched by the esky and made them fresh drinks. They clinked glasses again and sat drinking in the view. The pink and mango sky was streaked with deep purple, the sea now dark blue metal. The light kept changing, the shape of the clouds too. It was like being in a beautiful painting that was moving incrementally, the tones growing ever darker.

He slipped in behind her, legs on either side, and she sweetly sighed as they cuddled. He ran his hands slowly, almost absentmindedly, over her smooth thighs, and she turned to him, and they had a slow, delicious pash.

Coming up for air, they sipped their drinks and watched the sunset. It was dreamy, beatific, beyond words. She leant back; he looked down at her luscious body. He knew that she could feel him now, pressed hot against the small of her back.

"Isn't this better than anything?" said Cath.

"I reckon," said Seth.

He put his face down to hers, and they kissed again. He gently squeezed her breasts and caressed her tummy. She squirmed, moaned, and he went lower, rubbing through the cotton of her shorts, his fingers in the groove, teasing the hard little berry there.

"Do you want to do it now?" said Cath.

Seth hopped up and put their glasses on top of the esky. He squatted next to her and took her hand.

"Listen, Cath, let's do it in a . . . a certain way."

Her eyes went wary, so he got on his hands and knees and faced the sea. He stuck his bum out and looked over his shoulder at her. Her eyes ran over him in surprise and appreciation.

"You go into this possie," he said.

"Aye? And what are you going to do?"

"I'll be behind you."

"Behind me?" She didn't look so tickled at that.

"No funny business. Just the normal way."

She thought about it.

He held an imaginary crouching Cath around her hips.

"I'll be like this, and I'll have this." He held the packet up. "And when you're ready, you tell me to pop it on."

Cath stared at him, then burst into laughter.

"Is this so we can both look at the view?" she said.

"Yeah! Yeah, you got it. That's right."

Cath laughed again. "Well, isn't that thoughtful."

Giving him a cute look, she got on her hands and knees and faced the water. Seth gulped, almost squeaked, and moved in to kneel behind her. He stroked her legs and hips as they looked at the panorama around them.

Then they simultaneously broke into laughter, feeling the perfect, mad audacity of the moment.

"You're fun," said Cath, and she stood and stripped, her top and shorts falling to the sand. Then she got back on all fours again. Eyes popping, Seth gasped, marvelling at the curves of her legs and back and hips and bottom. He was a very lucky boy.

He dropped his shorts, suited up his old fella, and with a stroking hand prepared the way. Cath shivered, gasped, and arched her back. Then her hand was there too, and he put his hands on her hips and let her put him inside her. He gasped and followed her lead, working diligently on his counterstroke, but they began speeding up and were soon tumbling headlong into climax.

"Wait, wait," said Cath, and he stopped – but stayed in. Getting sand on the condom would put a proper brake on things. Maybe even end it.

"Let's not go off the deep end so fast," said Cath.

Leaning over, he put his face next to hers and slid back in. Nice and slow, they fired it up again. Ooh-ing and ahh-ing, cheek to cheek, they wallowed in pure sensation, the immensity of the place amplifying their pleasure, and for a few crazy moments it felt like there was just one mind in their two heads.

They kept it afloat, but it just got too good. Hearing it in his voice, she raced him, butting backwards, blonde head bobbing madly, and they crossed the line together with a resounding yell. Seth felt a starburst of impossible beauty, of something exquisite and sublime. It was as though a perfection, an ideal, had become real. He felt heavenly, he felt godlike.

They fell to the rug, laughing, gasping. They kissed and hugged face-to-face, and it was the icing on the cake. Then they stretched out, feeling the drug of sex ebb away, and listened to their breathing slow. Cath sighed, reached out and held his arm, and they watched the deep blue above them finally go black.

Lying under the stars, listening to the rasping chime of

the sea on the coral sand was mesmerising. After a bit they sat up. He saw it first, but he waited for her to notice, and when she did, her voice squeaked in delight.

"Look!" she cried. "At the edge of the water!"

The shoreline flickered with light as each wave broke onto the sand. The sea was full of phosphorescence, and all the way up the spit, silvery sparks and ripples danced.

"Oh wow, Seth!" said Cath. "Let's go in."

She stood and ran into a splash of pure light. She dived under in an explosion of neon bubbles, and he saw her moving underwater, the luminescence lighting her body. It was the most amazing thing to see – a space-age angel, an electric goddess – and he knew he'd never forget it.

He jumped in, and they splashed and plunged about in delight. Cath ran her arms through the water, lifting them in a spray of diamonds, the stars bright above and behind her. Seth stood, unleashing waterfalls of light, then made neon explosions, thumping his fists into the water. They laughed wildly. It was magical.

They kneeled face-to-face, arms around each other, and had a good, long kiss. Then with a hoot of hilarity, Cath pushed him back in the water, and he fell onto his heels, white fire bursting around him. Cath jumped onto his lap, wrapping her legs around him. Something quickly came up between them, and she gasped as they touched down there. With his head in her hands, she kissed him deeply, then pressed her face against his cheek.

Over her shoulder, Seth saw a big swirl of light in the water five metres away, something cleaving through the sea, a wide, dark shape lit by its own phosphorescence – rushing straight at them.

Holding her, he leapt up, did a one-eighty, and ran up the sand. Exploding through quicksilver, he felt the tip slip in and heard her squawk. Dry sand underfoot now, he let her down, turned, and saw the dark sea – then a flicker of light moving away, a fin or a tail breaking the surface.

"My God, what was that?" gasped Cath.

"Something sniffing around."

"You think it was going to eat us?"

"You'd hope not, hey."

Cath laughed. "Well listen, I want to eat *you*."

"Let's make a fire first," he said.

"What, you scared now?"

"Nah, I wanna see you in the nuddy again."

"Hah," said Cath, sounding pleased.

They gathered driftwood, lit a fire, and, what a clever girl, she had another frenchie. It was as good as the first time, but faster. They went all stops out and blew off like little volcanoes. Then with endorphins turning them into happy blobs of goo, they lay back on the rug and floated in a cloud of absolute contentment.

The waves hissed on the sand. A seabird called, its keening cry close by in the darkness. Seth got up and tended the fire. Cath lit a cigarette, and he was pleased she didn't put clothes back on. He liked sitting around with naked girls.

"You ever see a movie called Age of Consent?" he said, now remembering the title.

"Sounds like one of those sexy ones," said Cath.

"Yeah, it's pretty sexy," said Seth. "They made it over there on Dunk Island." He pointed out towards the Family Group. "And at Cardwell and Mission Beach."

"True?"

"Yeah. It's a good movie."

"Because it's sexy."

"Well, yeah, but also because –"

A great roar came from the sky in the northeast, a deep rumbling that swiftly grew in volume, and a long mass of cumulus cloud lit up from inside with a huge flame.

"Seth?" There was terror in Cath's voice. "What's that?"

The light dimmed, the unearthly noise swiftly fading, and the clouds flickered back to darkness.

Cath laughed madly. "Oh God, I nearly wet myself! That was like something from the Bible. What *was* that? One of those UFOs?"

"You never know," said Seth, a touch shaken himself. He had no bloody idea what they'd just seen.

"God, it all happens with you, doesn't it?" said Cath. "You turn up at North Shepard and then –"

"You hungry?" he said.

She made a hugely interested sound.

"What have you got?"

"Steak sandwiches with fried onions?"

She let out a burst of incredulous laughter.

"Or I could catch a fish," he said.

Cath groaned happily. "You watch out – I'll marry you."

Suntory Cowboy

In the early morning sun they had a nice, long kiss on the resort beach, then Cath wordlessly took his hand and led him up the sandy track to a little road.

"So, when are you coming back?" she said after a bit. "I can get some days off next week."

Yep, chicks don't muck around when they don't want to muck around, thought Seth. Last night had been fantastic, but truth be told, he wanted to do his own thing right now and in his own time. He didn't want to be organised.

Though there was never certainty with the weather, he had a plan: to circumnavigate the island, fish hard the last day coming up the channel, fill the empty cold box with his catch, and ice it up at Cardwell.

He had a mate, a grader driver on the road crews, who was renting a property outside of South Johnston. There was a little bungalow there that he could base himself at while the nonsense in Cairns blew over. Filling his mate's chest freezer with fish would be a good start.

"Yeahh . . ." he said uncertainly. "I've sort of got some things on. Maybe in–"

"Right." She cut him off, her eyes on the ground. He stopped. She stopped, her face blank. He took her by the shoulders and looked into her eyes.

"Listen, I'll be back. True. Last night was tops. It was like a . . . like a movie."

"The sexy one on Dunk Island?" she said.

"Nah, it was better than the movie."

She smiled and put her hand out. He took it, and they walked along, swinging their arms in silence.

The front side of the resort appeared through the forest: the covered verandah of the restaurant and bar and the corrugated tin roof of the building behind it. It all looked pretty small, and they soon passed it, descending through the trees and coming out at the jetty and shed that Seth had seen the day before.

In the morning light, the sea was glassy. There was no horizon, just half of Goold Island, the mainland ranges, and the western tip of Hinchinbrook glowing in the sun. Fifty metres out were the two yachts he'd seen the other day, their dinghies now tied to the sterns.

Moored at the jetty were a 12-footer and 20-footer in reasonably good nick, likely the resort's runabouts. The shed sat on a gravelled pad; behind it the cliffs of the cape rose steeply. In the shed, Ted, a nut-brown old nugget of a bloke, was working on a 20 HP Mercury outboard.

Cath said he was the Mr. Fixit who kept the resort from falling apart, and he changed the lightbulbs too. He was an affable bloke, and if not for his greasy hands, he would've shaken Seth's hand.

Cath introduced them, then she squeezed Seth's arm. They locked eyes, silly smirks rising on their faces, then she quickly turned and just about skipped out of the shed.

Ted pretended he hadn't seen anything, and while he worked, they talked about Seth's plans for travelling down the east coast of the island. When Seth asked if he could buy fuel if he needed it, Ted told him he had six forty-four gallon drums coming on the barge from Cardwell, so he could have whatever he needed whenever he wanted.

"And at standard price," said Ted as he clinked through some spanners. "The same as what you'd pay in Cardwell. No more than that." He looked at Seth.

"What sorta boat you got?"

Seth told him, and he thought about it.

"Yeah, fourteen foot and forty horsepower's okay. Just watch the weather, aye. You get some good swell on the ocean side, big waves popping up from nowhere too."

"I'll be right," said Seth.

"You make sure you are," said Ted. "Because there's no one round there. Not a soul."

The sea was silvery, the mountains ahead like a row of tiger shark teeth. He hadn't been bullshitting Cath about what a great time he'd had and that he'd be back, but it was great to be back on the water again, just racing along.

It had taken less than an hour to pass North and South Shepherd and clear the granite dome of Cape Sandwich. Finally heading south, with the island spread out in front of him, his adventure was now properly kicking off.

And besides, it wasn't that far from his mate's place in South Johnstone to come here. Visiting Cath would sure sweeten his exile from Cairns. He'd need his own boat, though, and maybe when the crop money came through he could look around for one.

With a glittering splash, a dolphin broke the sea ahead, and he thought of the incessant din the Evinrude must make underwater. A minute later a pod of dolphins cut in front of him, and he slowed down until they'd pissed off.

Past the cape, a vast expanse of beach unfolded. From the map, Ramsay Bay looked to be seven kilometres long, a thin line of trees and coastal scrub on a barrier dune. In some places the sand isthmus was only a few hundred metres wide; behind it were the creeks of Missionary Bay.

Tacking at times so as not to be completely side-on to the waves, he got halfway down Ramsay before turning towards the beach. Rowie had said the beach was known for beachcombing, its length and longshore drift trapping all manner of flotsam and jetsam from the Coral Sea.

He landed and chucked in the anchor. On the beach, the sand stretched away in a salt-laced haze. There were no palms or pretty flowers here, just spinifex, stalky grass, and nets of hardy, green creeper. The endless barrier dune rising up from the high-tide line was topped with soldier bush, wind-sheared casuarinas, and gnarly little acacias.

He pulled on rubber-soled canvas shoes and put on his floppy hat. With the binoculars and a full canteen of water in his shoulder bag, he ambled up the beach, rubber soles squeaking on the sand. Roughly keeping to the high tide line, he scrutinised the beach all the way down to the water's edge, his eyes alert for a worthy prize.

Amongst the usual beach litter of coral, shells, pumice, and driftwood, there were plastic and timber items. Right in front of him: a blue spoon, a red bucket cracked apart, a small white float with frayed rope attached, and other scraps of discarded colour. Give it another fifty years, and the beach would be a rainbow of crap.

But on a beach this long, the law of averages meant he'd find something interesting eventually; it was just a matter of how far he walked along it.

Beachcombing was something you'd normally do with a girlfriend or family: not exactly dull, but not much chop either. But he didn't mind it – the stroll, the discovery, and the cool stuff he'd find. Like the knife blade of good steel stuck fast in a slimy, barnacled plank that he'd cleaned up and made an ironwood handle for. Or the pair of quality swimming goggles in a cool case embossed with Japanese characters. And the perfect, unchipped nautilus shell, the green turtle skull, and the little, grinning, red monkey made of worm-holed wood.

He'd found all kinds of useful stuff, too: hand reels complete with lines, hooks, sinkers, and lures; lengths of good rope; jerry cans with lids; and things like what was in front of him right now – a two-litre plastic bottle with the top cut off and the handle still attached: someone's homemade bailer.

Ranging down to the wet sand, he walked over star-like patterns that went on as far as the eye could see: tiny balls of sand excavated by a million ghost crabs. The sweet stink of decay alerted him to empty cray heads and gutted crabs. There were also corpses of dollar fish, but they were too small to really pong.

Walking the high-tide line where a half-buried log had backfilled with tidal debris, he found an old blue glass bottle stopper with some etched letters still visible on it. That was a keeper. The second run on the board, a few minutes later, was the tiny fossil of a crab, the crustacean etched in perfect detail.

The beach was endless. It felt like anything might end up on it one day. But what he really wanted to find were those basketball-sized glass fishing floats, the blue, green, or transparent spheres bound with knotted rope netting. They were cool things that everyone wanted to hang from their verandahs or backyard bars. Some blokes sold them to tourists and collectors from the cities.

A roughly geometrical shape caught his eye: a wooden dinghy, hull up, buried flush to the sand. But from bow to stern, half of it was missing, like it had been perfectly cut down the middle. Crouching down by the weathered hull, he dug beside the keel and immediately felt wood. Using the side of his hand, he exposed the raised strip of a strake, then a patch of the hull. It was bloody strange, but the whole boat was there.

What sort of hydrodynamics had perfectly covered half the dinghy with a few centimetres of sand? The odds of it seemed scarcely possible, but nature had her ways. He'd seen enough crazy things to know that not everything was explainable with science or logic. Wishing he'd brought a camera, he walked on.

And how was this for more bizarreness? Sitting there on the sand like a bad joke was a pink, plastic cowboy hat, like something you'd win at a sideshow alley stall.

He picked up the befouled and scaly thing and squeezed it on over his own hat. It was a silly thing to do, but there wasn't any bastard around to see. He yee-hawed loudly, laughed at himself, then went back to beachcombing.

Sun glittered on glass, and he saw in the high-tide scree a bottle capped with a lid. It looked like it hadn't been in the water very long. He picked it up, and inside, nice and dry, was a rolled-up piece of paper. He twisted the lid off and used a stick to get the paper out. Unfolding it, he read the message – *Marooned. Send beer and women.* With a grunt of disappointment, he let the message flutter away and threw the bottle up past the high-tide line.

A few minutes later he found another bottle. Squat and dark green, it was embossed with the words 'Old Suntory Japanese Whisky.' Encrusted with marine growth, there was liquid in the bottom – three fingers' worth of amber fluid. It took his knife and a bit of oomph to get the lid off. He took a sniff, and hot fumes filled his nostrils. It was whiskey alright, and he took a sip. It tasted okay, so he had a swig and felt it burn down through his chest.

Some drunk Jap fisherman must have dropped it over the side. Maybe he'd gone in too. There were a lot of the bastards out there fishing where they bloody well liked, so he wasn't gonna cry if one of them ended up as fish food.

He took another hit. Sun-hot, it was like rocket fuel. He grinned at the sweep of bright sand. The grog was making him tingle. Upturning the bottle, he sucked down the last of it, then threw it up past the high tide line to thump onto the sand.

Wiping his lips, he grinned like a pirate king. Out here on Hinchinbrook Island, he was going feral. Buzzing away now, he eagerly scouted the radiant sand. There could be more grog, drugs, or even treasure! This goofy optimism made him chuckle.

The beach began to light up. Even with his sunnies on, it was dazzling, the sky pulsing bluer than blue, the sea rolling with billions of specks of light. Wonderfully giddy, legs suddenly weightless, he felt he was drifting upwards, like he could walk right up into the shimmering hot air. Almost stumbling, he regained his footing and laughed madly. Gee whillikers, the grog had gone right to his head!

In wild inebriation he began sprinting along the sand like a kid with a litre of red cordial onboard. Sand hissed and sprayed as he ran; sweat stung his eyes. He was a wild animal now, mindless and free. He was off the leash, on the loose, beyond the prison of thought or reflection, and it was great!

The upward drift returned, his feet coming right *off* the ground, and the blue hemisphere above reached down for him. For wonderful seconds he knew he was going to fly, but this time his stumble didn't stop, and he hit the beach and rolled over in the sand.

Gulping down air, he screamed with laughter. He was stupidly, hilariously pissed, and Jesus! What was this?

A gaunt figure stood over him – a Japanese fisherman in rotting shorts and a frayed and oil-stained tank top, his hollow, unshaven face without eyes, his head a mummy's skull grinning with nicotine teeth. Seth sat up in shock.

The apparition held out one bony hand for his whisky, fingers beckoning. Behind it, pieces of driftwood spiralled up and formed a swaying figure with smooth grey arms and an outsized mackerel skull as its head.

Desiccated dollar fish twitched into wriggling life, their empty eye sockets watching. Fossilised crabs the size of kelpies burst through the sand, carapaces like burnished armour, mouthparts moving in interlocked precision.

Grunting with alarm, Seth scrambled to his feet. The fisherman evaporated into thin air, the crabs too, and in a sudden reek of brine and diesel, a skeletal form brushed by him, or through him, the ghost of another poor bastard lost at sea. Further up the beach, through the salty haze, he saw more shapes wandering in the shallows, dozens of departed souls caught in the endless tides, rips, and winds of Ramsay Bay.

Dazed, he picked up his hats and put them back on. The wind made a high wailing sound, and he saw timber ribs of boats and jagged sheets of rusted steel plate rise up out of the sand – parts of shipwrecks like giant headstones for long-dead crews. He knew none of this was real, but it sure as hell felt like it was.

On a driftwood log, he plonked down to take a breather. He'd been drunk lots of times, but never like this. Sitting on the silvery wood, thankful for his long-sleeved shirt and the shade of his hat, he focused on breathing deeply. Concentrating on the vibrating horizon, he waited for all the things moving around the beach to disappear.

When they did, he got up. As he began to walk, feeling a wobble in his step, an immense boom, the loudest thing he'd ever heard in his life, blew him off his feet. Absolutely physical, this sonic fist king-hit him hard, and as he fell to the sand, he looked up.

A few hundred metres above, a huge machine flashed by, sharp and slick as a killing knife. It had a long, pointed nose, swept-back wings; then it was gone, its sonic boom echoing off the peaks of the island.

He lay there stunned, feeling the primal fear of an animal hunted. He saw newsreels in his head, people running from warplanes. He saw that naked Asian kid in the photo, running burnt and screaming along a highway.

Sitting up, he shouted defiance at the empty blue sky. There was a RAAF base south of here in Townsville, and hadn't they got those new Yank jets last year – the F-111s? Yeah, right, he'd just been buzzed by one of them.

Now he remembered the great roar and the flames he'd seen last night with Cath. That was no UFO – it was one of these bastards lighting up the sky.

Suddenly sluggish after all the excitement, he just sat there. When he looked down the beach for the Starcraft, he couldn't see it. He must have walked a long bloody way.

Peeling the cowboy hat off, he chucked it away, stupidly thinking that the RAAF pilot must be laughing at him for wearing it. Pulling his hat down tight, he stomped back along the beach, pissed-drunk and sweating hard. He attempted beachcombing, but his mind was reeling, so he concentrated on walking, one footstep after another.

He had drained his water bottle by the time he got to the boat, and a dirty little hangover now enveloped him. The Suntory had gone through him like a dose of salts.

Downing a couple of Aspro, he put a wet towel around his head, then continued south in the Starcraft. Down the end of Ramsey Bay he could see an isolated fang of rock sticking up a few hundred metres, the triangular granite plug like a practice model for the big peaks behind it.

At the end of the bay, he turned towards the sand and saw that there was another beach just beyond, a tiny cove between two low headlands, and he drove to it. Close to the first headland, a reef appeared, making a channel into the cove. Cruising in, he saw fish dart into the coral and a stingray fly across the wave-scalloped sand.

He anchored in the bay and sat for a moment checking it out. He'd got to the island proper now, the triangular peak right there by the beach, and beyond it, a wall of rugged ridges and castle-like outcrops rising up into the central mountain range of the island.

Shaped by wind, cloud obscured the tops of the peaks, and he flashed on the Pink Floyd album he'd found in the bargain bin at Chandlers Music Bar, a soundtrack to some movie set in the jungles of Papua New Guinea. He hadn't seen the movie, but, man, David Gilmour's guitar playing had really made him sit and notice the bloke.

He dug out the map in its clear plastic sleeve and found the outrider of rock he'd landed beneath – Nina Peak. It sounded like a chick's name, sort of black leather and rock'n'roll, and he resolved to climb it. Later. Still feeling a bit squiffy from the whisky, he needed a nap, and he went and took one in the shade of the trees on the beach.

It felt strange when he woke up. Having a sleep in the daytime was something he never did, something he'd be ashamed to admit. But what the hell? He was on holiday, and he could do whatever he liked.

The sludge of the hangover had gone, and he was ready for Miss Nina Peak. Just above the beach he soon found the track and followed it south, walking through open forest until he saw a narrow ridge running up the side of the peak. It was easy enough following this razorback, with faintly worn stones in the earth showing that people had been coming up here for a long time.

Twenty minutes later he was at the summit looking out at the big view. He could see the next two beaches along, and they didn't look so far – five minutes by boat at the most. To the north, ten kilometres away, were a row of sunlit hills separating Shepard and Ramsay Bays, and in deep afternoon shadow, the expanse of Missionary Bay writhed with the silver snakes – the creeks reflecting light as they cut through the mangroves.

Clambering along scrub-covered rock and through low, dense bushes, he squeezed around to the southern edge of the peak, wary of loose stones and the sheer drop by his feet. Edging carefully past weathered blocks of granite and gnarly, unyielding branches, he finally found a spot where he could stop and look out to the north.

Everything lay in shadow, with sunlight bouncing up in sheets and rays over the peaks and valleys of the range. The massif was dark and ancient, and white dots moved across it: cockatoos a kilometre away, their calls echoing faintly off plunging cliffs and rock towers.

Crouching there with the wilderness before him, Seth flashed on the chick in King Kong – tied-up and presented to whatever it was that was waiting out in the jungle – and for a wild moment he imagined a giant hairy hand coming out of the trees below and plucking him right off the peak.

Back at the boat, he took a squizz at the map again, then drove south to the next bay. Unsurprisingly, it was called Nina Beach, and that sounded like the chick with the cool sports car in one of those European movies.

The mountains hovered over the beach, and there were boulders like giant marbles at the northern end. He saw coconut trees and a creek fed by a lagoon. It all looked most hospitable. Dropping anchor, he checked the creek, and in the clear water he saw – yum, yum, yum – some mud crabs.

Using the last of the bait, he chucked a crab pot in, then took his rod to the creek mouth. Within five minutes he'd caught a flathead. He made a fire, fried the fillets up in butter, and with tomato, iceberg lettuce, bread and butter, and a dollop of Mum's lime pickle, it was perfect.

Sitting comfy on the sand, eating with his fingers off the enamel plate, he felt bloody grateful. If he were a religious type, he might have more to say about it, but right here, right now, it was enough just to feel blessed.

As he cleaned up, squatting by the water and using sand to scour the frying pan, a deep rumbling came from the great pluton of rock behind him. It sounded like thunder or an avalanche of rocks, and he jumped up and looked back at the mountains. The sky was clear, the black peaks still. He listened for a bit longer but heard nothing more.

The Big Picture

Clouds sailed across the dawn sky. A sou-easter had picked up, and dry leaves rattled over sand and rocks. Up in the forest behind the beach, birds called. Seth got up, wandered down to the water, and looked back. The great massif was scrubbed clean, not a speck of cloud anywhere, the crags all glowing in the morning sun.

It looked rugged as hell up there. He knew the ranges had been climbed by locals and Townsville-based troops on jungle training, but there was no way he was doing anything like that. He was here to relax, not bust his arse.

There were two muddies in the crab pot, and he quickly boiled them in seawater. Cracking the crustaceans apart, he ate them with the last of the butter. After washing up, he sorted the esky, pouring out the water and putting the most perishable stuff around the shrinking block of ice.

Everything to do with food got wiped and packed away tight. Roaming the bush were scaly-tailed rats with chisel-sharp teeth. They'd gnaw through anything if they smelt food: even concrete. Bloody big bastards, some went to a kilo in weight, and they were no fun to corner or surprise.

Zoe Bay, the beach of his teenage memories, was the next bay, less than half an hour away. He knew what going into the bay by boat would be like: he'd seen that postcard view. So why not walk in and come out of the bush right *into* the picture? He'd be in the movie, not looking at it.

From the map, he saw he'd have to skirt a big mangrove swamp to come out at the southern end of the bay, but it wouldn't take more than a couple of hours, and the terrain was mostly flat. Easy stuff. Not like climbing mountains.

He loaded his rucksack with a canteen, a long-sleeved shirt, spare socks, the last of the fruit, and his floppy hat. Then he pulled his bush knife from its scabbard. It was a WW2-issue Machet 15 with a bolo blade of Port Kembla steel and a cross-hatched, brown Bakelite handle.

The buffalo-leather scabbard was stitched to one side of the rucksack so that the bush knife's handle stuck up over his left shoulder. It was a bit Z Force, but for hiking in the bush it was more than practical. No snagging on branches or bouncing against his leg. And if needed, quick to draw.

He took the marijuana with him, just in case. It seemed unlikely that park rangers or, God forbid, cops, would find his boat and search it, but he didn't want to even chance it. Even with the little he had, he'd get banged up in jail.

Boots on, he used his t-shirt as a shoulder pad to drag the boat up in under the branches of some gnarly beach almonds at the tree line. Only some nosey parker coming into the bay and scanning with binoculars would see it.

And just in case there were boat thieves around, he pulled the spark plug from the Evinrude, put it in a plastic bag, and hid it under a rock a little way into the trees.

Slipping the rucksack on, he tightened the straps. His arm flashed as he quick-drew the Machet, its grip filling his hand like a mate's handshake. He held the blade out, steady as, then, with a practiced left hand guiding, slid it back into the scabbard. Repeating the move, he laughed. You comic-book hero, he told himself.

He took the track south again, passing Nina Peak, and was soon in a valley. This trail down the east coast didn't look like it got much use. Any local would come to the island by boat. Trudging along a sweaty track through the bush was for surveyors, army boys, nature freaks, and the National Parks stiffs paid to do it.

On either side of the track, slopes rose up a few hundred metres. The valley turned into a saddle, and at its highest point he stopped to take in the view. The blue curve of Zoe Bay went in under a range of jungle hills, but there was no horizon; the hill on the left blocked any view of the sea.

Mangrove swamp lurked behind the bay, and in it he glimpsed the curve of a large creek. Behind the mangrove was tall forest studded with massive paperbarks and other swamp trees, then a couple of square kilometres of what looked like palms. He knew that the central range and the big valley running through it were right there, but, damn, the hills to the right of the saddle blocked the view.

To get the big picture, he needed elevation. He began climbing the slope next to him. It was easy going, and he soon came out on a high, sedgy ridge. Taking his pack off, he gazed out at the grandest bit of bush he'd ever seen.

In the south, a mountain range rippled by countless deep valleys filled the sky, with one peak towering up over the rest: the nearly kilometre-high Mount Diamantina. And, wow, there was *another* big range behind it. To the west, just a few kilometres away, Mount Bowen and The Thumb crowned their own range of peaks. Looking very jagged and rugged up close, they were big buggers. On the map, Mount Bowen was over a kilometre high, and The Thumb came in a smidge below Mount Diamantina.

Seth shook his head in awe. This was a panorama worth bringing a camera for. He got out the binoculars and took in a fishing eagle's view of Zoe Bay. Below him, a huge sandbar bordered the mouth of a wide creek, the pristine blue and white of it spellbinding. The creek, more of a river really, was fed by a big lagoon enclosed by mangrove swamp. With the steep ranges surrounding the bay, the runoff into the creek in the wet would be enormous.

Zoe Bay was two kilometres long, and at its farthest end he saw a strip of beach. Focusing in, he saw the white sand had a sharp edge: the mouth of the southern creek. From the map and what Rowie had said, there was a waterfall a few hundred metres up the creek with a good swimming hole and more pools above it. He'd be sweaty when he got there, but he didn't mind working for a swim: it always made it nicer.

Behind the bay, the big valley went up steeply between the ranges. On its slopes were rock outcrops sticking up above the jungle and smaller valleys choked with trees.

Climbing back down, he found the track at the saddle and descended into forest. It was open in places, but he could see big trees, massive specimens of stringy bark and bloodwood that you could build a street of houses from.

After a bit, he came to a wide creek full of rocks and boulders. There was a good stream of water in it, and he guessed this was the main arm of the big creek he'd seen from above the saddle. Boots and socks off, he picked his way through the cool water, the rocks slippery underfoot.

Further up the creek there was a dark pool splashed with neon-bright blobs of sunlight, and, with a shock, he saw people sitting there, dark-skinned, almost naked. In reflex, he nodded in greeting, but there was no one there, only shadows, and he laughed at his vivid imagination.

Some new friends began buzzing around his head, and after an Aerogard stop, he walked on, now with a feeling that the track was finally curving in behind the bay. He crossed another creek, dry and filled with boulders. With no canopy overhead, the jumble of stone was hot and bright. Sweat trickled down his ribs as he went from rock to rock, a few moving as he stepped on them. Crikey, he thought, you wouldn't want to break your ankle here.

Halfway across, he saw how steeply the creek went up the valley. It looked like a path for giants. On the other side he had to look for the track, but he soon found it. The ground was dark with the humus of the forest; the track a lighter line of debris trod into powder over the decades.

Padding through the cool gloom, he could hear the sound of parrots excitedly feeding somewhere. The forest felt untouched and ancient, but then he saw the turret of a big tree stump, its mossy wood pocked with notches for footholds: a reminder of when the island was a timber-cutter's paradise.

Palm trees began to crowd the canopy, their trunks like the columns of a lost city. There were Alexandra, Halifax, and solitaire palms, many thirty or more metres high. He stopped for a moment and just stared. They were the biggest palms he'd ever seen.

Sunlight streamed down between them, lighting up huge golden orb spider webs and the dead birds cocooned in them. Walter had said everything was big here, thought Seth. There'd have to be some huge pythons about.

It felt muffled, the air unmoving. His footsteps seemed

muted. As he walked, wait-a-while, calamus, and Atherton palms mobbed the track, plucking at him with hooks and spiny fronds. Ducking and twisting past them, he stayed alert for any insects leaping onto him.

The palm forest went on for a good way, and when it began to recede, the ground became squishy underfoot. Sedge and moss began to edge the track, and up ahead he now saw tea trees, swamp paperbarks, and cabbage tree palms. Bloody hell, he'd come to a melaleuca swamp.

There'd be no sense of where the track was in there, just pools of fetid water, tussocks of saw-sedge, submerged roots, and drowned logs. He'd have to find it on the other side. Walking into the swamp, the smell of dead water and decaying vegetation made his nose wrinkle, and, damn it, his boots and socks went soggy straight away. He didn't mind roughing it, but the thought of the rancid swamp juice marinating his feet really gave him the pip.

Five metres in, he stopped and looked back at where he'd come from. There were two fairly straight trees side-by-side, and he took a mental snapshot of them.

He splashed past palm tree suckers and button orchid-draped melaleucas. He saw the vivid blue flash of a sacred kingfisher taking flight. Insects dive-bombed him as he avoided big logs and clambered over massed roots.

Eventually he got to the other side. He had to piss about looking for the track, and when he found it, he walked back to the swamp, then went in five metres, turned, and took another mental picture. Now he had some idea of where the track entered and exited the swamp.

Walking along to the squelchy accompaniment of his boots, he began to see blue paperbark, turpentine, and wattle. Soon he was in the coastal forest behind the beach. Twenty minutes later he saw a swampy creek, its edges webbed with mangrove roots and clusters of nipa palms. Things leapt and plopped at his approach. He knew from the map that the creek was the furthest tributary of the big lagoon.

He passed the creek, and soon the light grew brighter in the canopy. He heard the wind rustling the tops of the trees now, then the faint roar of the sea. Ten minutes later he came out into the glare of the beach. He checked the Submariner, and just like he'd calculated, walking to Zoe Bay had taken just over two hours.

He looked out at the water and saw that the horizon was surprisingly short. The headlands framing the bay were several kilometres long, but they curved in, especially the northern one. The mouth of the bay was smaller than the length of the beach. It looked almost cosy.

The southern creek was less than half a kilometre away; the other side of it mangroves, then forested hills. To the north the beach stretched away, and at its far end was the white streak of the big sandbar he'd seen.

Finding a shady spot under some sheoaks, he took off his pack and drank some water. As the sweat dried, he contemplated checking out the big creek and lagoon at the far end, then decided that going in there later with the Starcraft was the smarter thing to do.

The tide was out some way, and he saw how shallow the bay was, its length and width like an airstrip. He walked down to the water and looked back at a swathe of emerald forest above a long line of white sand, and behind it, a solid wall of rocky peaks. Well here it is, he thought – the view just like I remembered it. I'm standing smack in the middle of a memory.

He went to the creek, its mouth curving around a rocky point as it entered the bay. You'd need a good high tide to get in by boat, but it soon widened to a small anchorage.

At the creek mouth was a grove of trees: beach almonds and matchbox beans, and when Seth walked in amongst them, he could see by the specks of carbon and paper and foil in the sand that this was the camp spot.

At the edge of the grove, down a gentle sand slope, was the creek. Under the trees he saw a pad of beaten earth heading into the bush: the track, and he followed it along the creek. The watercourse quickly narrowed, revealing rocks and races that would deter any saltwater predators. After a few hundred metres, a waterfall appeared through the trees. Running like white lace across a twelve-metre-high rock face, it fed a big pool of cool, luminous blue.

"Maate," breathed Seth.

Making his way over a shoreline of rocks, he saw logs stuck fast amongst boulders. This southern creek would also run with real force in the wet, with torrential water exploding over the falls. It would be a sight to see.

Out of his shorts and boots in seconds, he gratefully slid in, and, man, it was heaven. After spending a good half hour in the pool, with little jungle perch nibbling his toes, he got out, sat naked on a rock, and ate a mango. It was warm, and the insects loved him, so he got back in and swam about for a while longer.

After drying off in the sun, he put his shorts and boots back on. Rowie had said there were pools with a view of the bay just a short climb up the left side of the falls.

Shouldering his pack, he scrambled up a steep rocky slope, using the branches and bushes along the forest line to pull himself along. He passed a golden penda in flower, and amongst the vivid yellow blooms came a flash of brilliant neon blue as a Ulysses butterfly got itself a feed.

Above the falls were big slabs and seams of bare rock, the creek flowing along a series of small pools. Seth went to one by the falls and grinned from ear to ear. The view was an absolute pearler, one of those setups you always hoped to find in the bush.

From a hundred metres above the beach, he could see its white curve going all the way to the big sandbar in the distance. Above the sandbar, the hill-studded headland stuck out into the blue of the bay. It was too good.

He stripped off, slipped into the pool. Moving across to the edge, he leaned forward, put his arms on the sun-hot rock, and let his body float up in the cool water. He looked out at the vista and thought of Cath. He had to bring her here. She could lean forward in front of him, looking at the view too, and he could slide over her – and he just about had to slap his hand away.

The Submariner said it wasn't yet ten, so he went naked up the creek for a look-see. Dragonflies and moths zipped and fluttered as he wended his way over shelves of rock and through lillypilly and stunted bottlebrushes growing in the cracks alongside the running water.

Up ahead he saw something lying on a rock by a pool. Moving in slowly, he saw a goanna. From its head to its bumhole, it was a metre long; its tail close to double that. He paused. He'd never seen one this size, but he'd seen them rip apart dead or dying roos and cattle with their long sharp claws. And they had cousins who lived across the Arafura Sea on Komodo Island: beasts of truly King Kong dimensions that were not averse to eating humans.

He moved in closer, real slow, but the giant lizard saw him. With a rattle of claws it dived in, then swam towards the other side of the pool. Seth raced forward to see the long, speckled body undulating madly as it swam under the water. Seconds later it burst from the water, the rock splattering dark around it, and charged off into the scrub.

Impressed, Seth followed the creek again, careful to avoid any groin-level branches. He went past pools filled with pebbles and surrounded by gnarly trees with roots like melted wax extruding from the rock. It grew steeper, the creek coming down from a sharp-edged gully, and he heard water chuckling in narrow channels and drumming subsonic in hidden rock cavities.

Above the gully he climbed a crest of rock and heard the faint drone of a small outboard engine coming from the beach below. He had company.

A little intrigued, he went back along the creek to the falls. As he got closer, the sound stopped, and he surmised that someone had come ashore in a dinghy from a boat. He couldn't grumble, though; there were several billion people on the planet, and one or two of them had made it here.

Back at the pools, the cool water and view beckoned, and he had another swim. It was like being in a postcard, and he was glad it was remote and protected by the law. When he got out, he finished up the water in his canteen and refilled it from the pool. He got dressed, pulled on his rucksack, and wondered who had turned up.

It was probably some locals from Lucinda or Dungeness across the channel, but he was enjoying the solitude, and he'd meet them soon enough. So he crossed the creek, went into the bush, and began walking along a ridge that ran parallel to the beach. He'd seen this row of small hills on the map and reckoned it was worth a look. It was the only high ground behind the beach, everywhere else being coastal forest or mangrove swamp.

There wasn't much of a view of the beach or the creek from up here, the foliage too thick, but at times he got glimpses of the bay. Dodging around trees and bushes, hopping over rocks, he kept his eyes peeled for snakes and nests of biting insects. But what he really had his eye out for was a cave or a good-sized overhang of rock.

The island so far was pretty bloody nice, but Zoe Bay was something else. He'd be back, and a hidden spot off the beach and near the falls where he could store gear or even camp would suit him nicely.

As he traversed the ridge, cables and loops of liana and thickets of caper vine directed his passage. He came to a dry gully, a hot gash of rocks through the trees. Guessing that it ran back to the creek, he crossed the jumble of sunlit rocks and kept going.

The crest of a hill loomed thirty metres above him, and he ascended it. Looking further along the ridge, he saw nothing to suggest caves or outcrops of rock. But in the bush, that didn't always mean a lot. As his ex-army mate Les would say – just because you can't see it doesn't mean it isn't there.

Changing tack, he decided to examine the base of the ridge. Climbing down, he saw another dry watercourse running towards the beach. Following it down onto the flat, he began to amble along the base of the ridge. It was quiet; no wind or birdcalls, and, faintly at first, he heard a repetitive sound. Moving towards it, he listened hard. It sounded familiar. Then it stopped.

He stopped and waited and then saw some movement not thirty metres away. An electric shock went through his scalp, and he instinctively crouched down.

Someone was over there doing something, and the fact that they were doing it hundreds of metres from the beach meant it had to be something nefarious.

Dr Tarzan, I Presume

The sound started again. Metal on earth. Digging. Seth uncapped the binoculars, hung them from his neck. The sun in the forest made a static pattern of shadow and light he did not want to disturb, so he began moving ever so slowly towards the action.

Creeping in, he saw that the forest wasn't dense enough to disguise his movements. Another fifteen metres and he'd be seen. Coming to a halt, he gradually lifted the glasses to his eyes. Focusing in, he saw a suntanned man in a white singlet, but the low light and the placement of leaves and branches made other details hard to see.

Very bloody curious now, he looked around for cover to get closer. There was a large dead branch festooned with purple coral pea flowers, then a stand of she-oaks. That'd get him in another five metres or so.

With the sound of digging louder than his movements, he went in, ducking and crawling like a crafty monkey. Coming in behind the she-oaks, he copped the bottom of a golden orb web in the face, the big sticky thing strong. Rearing back, he saw from the corner of his eye the plate-sized spider scurry down onto his head.

Stifling a grunt, he felt its long legs skid off his sweaty scalp. Realising how big its prey actually was, the spider raced off. Skin crawling, head down, Seth tore through the web, his boots crackling on leaves. He froze, then slowly sank to his haunches and became very still. The digging continued, and bugs began to orbit his head. Nice and slow, he raised the binoculars to his eyes.

Through the trees he saw the muscular back of a man working with a shovel. He was of reasonable height, with longish hair, and Seth wondered if he was some sort of hippy or back-to-nature freak. It was unlikely out here, but you never knew with that mob.

The man shovelled a bit more, then crouched down. A couple of minutes went by. When he stood up, Seth tried to glass his face, but the fella wasn't even close to side-on. All that was visible was the edge of an unruly beard.

Then someone stood up next to him – a woman, equally suntanned, in a t-shirt, and probably a foot shorter. She'd been invisible, sitting while the man worked, and was also facing away from Seth. He heard the murmur of voices, then they disappeared into the trees in the direction of the beach.

Like a hungry owl, he kept his eyes riveted on the spot, while little winged bastards dive-bombed him and drank his sweat and blood. He gave it five long minutes before standing and moving forward. Brushing the bities away, his gaze didn't deviate from where he'd seen the couple.

When he got there, almost tripping over a log, he looked around and saw trampled seedlings, then angry ants on a freshly crushed, rotten branch. Getting on his hands and knees, he searched the ground and under the leaves and twigs and found freshly dug earth.

Crawling about carefully, he soon saw an edge to the disturbed ground, then another, and he quickly identified an area about half a metre square.

On a nearby acacia bush, he snapped the tip of a branch at face height and let it hang. He went to another acacia on the other side of the disturbed earth and snapped the end of a branch in the same way. Then he slowly moved away, looking all about as he went, intent on locking this neck of the woods into his head.

He quietly went through the forest to the beach. Just inside the tree line, he peeked out. He saw a white yacht anchored near the creek mouth, but the beach there and anyone on it wasn't visible from where he was.

Standing in shadow, he thought about what he'd seen. He knew that fishermen stashed fuel, nets, and supplies along the coast, but not that far from the beach. Thinking about it some more, he decided to walk up to the northern end of Zoe Bay. He'd go introduce himself to them later.

Keeping just out of sight in the trees, he picked his way through the bush. From time to time he looked back along the beach, and eventually he saw a black inflatable on the beach with two figures. Using the glasses, he made out the couple he'd seen before, the woman lying on her back on the sand, the bloke walking a little distance away. They both looked suntanned and fit, and he pegged them as yachties sailing along the Queensland coast.

He walked on, checking out the water every ten minutes or so for fishy action, and he saw some: schools of mullet in the gutters close to the shore, a good few unidentified splashes, and a pod of dolphins out towards the middle of the bay.

Finally he got to the end of the bay. The tide was way out, the exposed beach in scalloped rows, with sandpipers and plovers down at the water's edge. The sandbar beach stuck out fifty metres into the bay, its white glare edging the deep blue channel where the enormous creek entered the bay. On the other side of the channel, the ground rose steeply from mangrove into a range of hills and turret-like rock outcrops. It was a top spot.

At the creek mouth, the beach curved inland, and Seth followed it onto a small back beach. Now he could see the full expanse of the river mouth lagoon there. It was a few hundred metres long, the water a deep, cool green, and there was space to park a lot of boats. Relinquishing the rucksack from his hot back, he drank water and looked around. Three stingrays basked by the water's edge, but there were no croc slides or tracks in the sand. It looked like no one had been here in months.

Lots of splashes in the lagoon meant there were lots of fish. Nice. High tide at night around the full moon, and you'd be piling them up on the sand. Spending a week here with a freezer-equipped cabin cruiser, then selling the catch in Cairns or Townsville, would be a good money spinner. He knew fellas who'd do that, national park or not. But not him. There were bigger things than money.

The view walking back was bloody nice. He really felt the place now, the grandeur of it growing by the hour. As he got closer to the creek and the yacht, he saw that the couple were sitting on the rubber side of their inflatable, a Zodiac-style dinghy with a 2 HP outboard.

They looked in their thirties, as fit as they'd appeared in the binoculars. As he approached, he saw that they were talking, sizing him up, and that was fair enough, as he was a bloke with a bush knife on a remote island beach. Out here anything could happen, and no one would ever know.

He gave them a good smile and was pleased to get good smiles in return. The woman's face was an interesting mix of soft and hard, with big brown eyes that seemed to take in everything around her. In shorts and t-shirt, she looked fit and trim, and pretty attractive too.

The bloke was a hairy beanstalk padded with muscle. He had a wild beard, hair to his shoulders, a stainless steel wristwatch on his wrist, and a silver ring in one ear.

"Dr. Tarzan, I presume," he said.

He spoke like a Yank, so it was a pretty funny thing to say, mixing up comics with British history. Seth laughed; it was the sort of silly thing his dad would say.

"Well, you must be . . ." Seth racked his memory and was pleased to remember it. "Stanley."

The man laughed. "Yeah, but I'm American, so I'd have to be Mouse or Owsley."

Okay, he's speaking English, thought Seth, but I'm not understanding a damn thing.

"A San Francisco joke, my friend."

"You're from there?" Well, that's cool, thought Seth.

"Yeah," said the bloke. His teeth appeared in his beard as a delighted smile. "On our last leg across the Pacific, then down to Sydney. Port Vila was our last port of call."

"Wow," said Seth.

The fella grinned. "Wild, huh?"

"So, how long does it take to get here from the New Hebrides?" said Seth, trying to imagine just how he'd go crossing the Coral Sea on a small yacht.

"Well, we had a storm a few days ago, thirty hours of big seas and wind. Put us off course, so . . . nearly nine days."

"This is Zoe Bay?" said the woman. She was a Yank too.

"Sure is," said Seth.

"It's so remote. I bet no one comes here."

"Aww, not many. I'd say only locals really."

"Not so popular with yachts, huh?"

"I've been on the island a couple of days, and I haven't seen one yet," said Seth.

The yachties nodded, waited for more.

"The army does exercises here," offered Seth.

"They do that often?" said the bloke.

Seth shook his head. "Maybe every few years. They'll hike, abseil down cliffs and gullies. But no live fire."

"Well, that's a relief," laughed the bloke.

"Yep, it's off the beaten track, the old Hinchinbrook."

"There's a waterfall here, right?" said the woman.

"Yeah," said Seth. "You haven't been up there yet?"

"No, but I can't wait. There's a pool to swim in, right?"

"There sure is. You'll see perch in there."

"Perch?"

"Yep, but they're too small to eat and it's national park here. There's bigger fish in the bay, and I've got a permit."

The Yank fella laughed, threw up his hands.

"And I've got two rods on the boat," he said.

Seth stuck out his hand. "I'm Seth."

"Jack," said the Yank.

As they shook, he said, "Like Jack London."

Seth felt jubilant; the name rang a bell.

"The white dog," he said, and they smiled at him.

Seth made teeth and jaws with his hand, opening and closing it. "White Fang, mush. Mush, mush!"

The Yanks laughed.

"All the way out here, you know that," said the woman.

She stuck out a slim hand. "Elinore."

Seth saw how completely self-assured she was in her gaze and stance. Like a bloke.

They shook, her grip confident, and she looked at him like she had a power he could only guess at. If this is what American women were like, then he didn't mind it at all.

"You here on your own?" said Jack.

Seth nodded, pointed north up the beach. "I'm camped a little further up the coast. Been up at the lagoon there all morning. I'm just hiking about having a look-see."

"A look-see?" Elinore smiled. "On your own?"

"That's right," said Seth, liking the look he got.

"Nobody lives on the island, huh?"

"Not really, but there's a resort on the northernmost tip of the island," said Seth. "It's called Nature Lovers."

The Yanks grinned at that.

"And that's it," said Seth.

"Lots of bugs?" said Elinore.

"You bet. They're not so bad on the beach, but there are places that will make you wish you didn't have skin."

"Malaria, dengue fever – stuff like that?"

"I hope not, but there's always the chance, aye. There's insects that'll lay jiggers under your skin that hatch right out of you." Seth suddenly felt like a tourist guide.

"You trying to put us off?" said Jack. "Well, too late, man, the Yanks are here!"

Seth laughed. The bloke was a joker.

"The fabled waterfall of Zoe Bay," said Elinore. "I've been hearing about it for years, and now here I am."

Seth dug that. She had her own dream of this place.

"Oh yeah, it's not far," said Seth. "I'll show you."

She clapped her hands together, somewhere between delight and command. "Lead on, Dr. Tarzan."

They all laughed, and Seth felt a giddy thrill. Everything had suddenly become larger than life, and he liked it.

He pointed to the grove of trees at the creek mouth. "We go through there."

As they walked, Elinore sighed happily at everything: the cool grove of trees, the creek with its little beach, the rock races of the creek. Jack, grinning like a big, furry kid, yakked about Zoe Bay's reputation amongst yachties. It was world famous. Though apparently not so crash hot as a long-term anchorage, it was worth spending a few days at: swimming at the falls, soaking up the scenery, and taking photos to show other yachties.

"The lie in that is – photographs always look so flat and puny. Like a machine has been given the task of showing you the place," said Jack. Beard in the air, he waved his arms up at the forest. "But it sure ain't this!"

Beaming with joy, Seth couldn't agree more.

As they came through the last of the trees, the falls and the big blue pool made Jack roar with appreciation. Seth loved it. An Aussie bloke would just go, 'Yeah, nice.'

"Oh lordy," said Elinore, and she began hopping across the rocks towards the water. Like a wild monkey, Jack followed. They got to the water's edge, stripped, and got in. With cries of delight, they splashed about.

Slightly uneasy, Seth took off his boots and socks. Nude with a chick or with old mates was cool, but it felt odd with a couple, strangers too, and he waited until Elinore had gone under before he dropped his shorts.

As quick as he could, he hopped across the rocks. Just

as he got to the water, Elinore surfaced nearby in a spout of water, her hands throwing her hair back from her face, her nipples dark, her stomach brown and flat. Banging his foot, Seth scrambled the last couple of steps. Crouching to slip into the water, he saw Elinore copping an eyeful.

It was odd. They were just naked; it didn't mean a thing, but there was something like an invitation in her eyes. He had to be careful. Misunderstandings about other blokes' women could be dangerous. Especially out here. And for all he knew, Jack might have a rifle on the yacht.

They all swam out into the pool, but as they approached the falls, Seth swam off. After days cooped up on a yacht, storm and all, he'd let them enjoy this by themselves.

Near the pool's edge, he flipped onto his back. Floating there with the sky overhead, he felt something eternal about this place. But when he tried to think about it and shape it in his mind, the beguiling awareness ebbed away.

Sneaking a look, he saw the Yanks were getting the vibe, cuddling in the water by the falls. He quietly swam to his shorts and boots, put them on, then took the lead back to the beach.

He hadn't been there long when Jack hurried out onto the sand and came over with a big smile on his face.

Well, that's nice, thought Seth. The bastard thought I was going to steal his yacht. America must be a rougher place than I'd thought.

"I thought you'd want some peace and quiet," said Seth.

Jack made a bow of appreciation that was somehow also an apology for being suspicious.

"You're a gentleman," he said, and Seth forgave him.

Then Elinore appeared on the beach and came walking

towards them. I bet she didn't think I was a thief, thought Seth. A big black figure came out of the forest behind her. As tall as a man, it was covered in shaggy hair and sported a blade-like helmet on its head.

"Ah, righty-o," said Seth, the tone of his voice making Jack turn to look.

"Jesus Christ!" said Jack. "What the fuck is that?"

"A cassowary." Seth began walking towards Elinore.

"Hey, Elinore," he called in a cheerful voice. "Don't run or anything, but we've got a mate. Keep coming, and we'll all go into the trees over here."

She turned and saw the big bird. "Oh, my God!"

"Man, look at those claws," gasped Jack.

Full of curiosity, the cassowary sped up. With a squawk of nervy laughter, Elinore turned and came towards them.

"Let's go in here, hey," said Seth, pointing at a stand of beach almonds, their long branches sticking out past the high tide line. "We'll take a peek at it from in there."

As the cassowary drew closer, they went amongst the tree limbs, some less than a metre off the sand. Crouching and ducking, they got into the middle of some horizontal branches. Full of curiosity, the animal followed them to where the low branches barred its big body and long legs.

Right in close, the nearly two-metre-high bird peered in at them, its eyelids blinking, its bright blue head bobbing, the huge pointed claws powdered with sand.

"See the curve of its tail?" said Seth. "It's a male."

"Wow, wow, wow," whispered Elinore.

"This sure ain't Sesame Street," said Jack happily.

Thank you, big bird, thought Seth. This is something they'll remember their whole lives. And I was with them.

The cassowary stuck its head through the branches, and the Yanks looked ready to burst with excitement. But they were savvy enough not to make any sudden moves or loud sounds. Instead, they watched in open-mouthed joy until the cassowary lost interest and wandered off, its long neck darting down as it checked out the beach.

In amongst the branches, they looked at each other and laughed, and Seth was more than happy to see what they'd all just shared shining in their eyes.

"Man! I didn't know a thing like that existed," said Jack, laughing with mostly feigned hysteria.

"Well, if that didn't look like a dinosaur," said Elinore. "The head, claws, the size of it. We know dinosaurs are related to birds, and, my God, this wonderful creature is an actual living missing link. And there's something else living here from the era of dinosaurs, right? Crocodiles.

"Yeah, probably," said Seth. "The channel on the other side of the island is where you're likely to see 'em. They got pretty much shot out along the coast and up the rivers. After a hundred years, there's not too many left."

"Oh, you poor Australians." Elinore pulled a face. "In another few years there'll be none left."

"Actually, no. There's a new law that finally made it to Queensland. It's an offense to kill them now," said Seth.

"Oh, you clever Australians."

"And it's been national park here since 1932. The whole island. Everything's protected."

"Very clever Australians."

"But we'll have to keep an eye out for that cassowary, though. For some reason he thinks it's his beach."

"Did you organise him to be here?" grinned Elinore.

Seth shrugged. "It's what Doc Tarzan does."

Grinning with happiness, he enjoyed their laughter.

They began walking to the inflatable, and Jack mimed drinking from a cup.

"Coffee?"

"Sure," said Seth. He was always up for something new.

"I'll go get the fixings. You sticking around, man?"

"Yeah, no rush," said Seth. It wouldn't take long to walk back to the Starcraft, then drive it around here.

"And breakfast?" said Jack. "We got some French baked beans, eggs. Onions too."

"Look, don't do anything on my account."

"What about a rug and some cushions?" said Elinore, and Jack bowed and scraped like a servant.

"Because I'm going to just sit down," she said, and she sat down and stretched out her legs. Jack began to speak.

"No, just . . ." said Elinore, gesturing at the inflatable.

Jack turned to Seth with a fixed smile and clapped his hands together. "See you in ten, man." He loped down to the inflatable and fired up the outboard.

Seth and Elinore watched him travel the ten metres out to the anchored yacht. The boat sure looked like it had come direct from America. It looked brand new.

"Lovely-looking boat," he said.

"Isn't it?" said Elinore. "Bob Weston design, launched last year. It's set up for two to sail it, but we had Joey crew with us from San Francisco to Port Vila. Jack had a nice old ketch, but he sold it. I've been sailing since I was a kid. I've had shares in a couple of yachts, but this one's mine."

Seth nodded attentively, but, dear God, the yacht just didn't look big enough to cross the expanse of the Pacific.

"Pretty small, hey?" said Elinore, like she knew what he was thinking.

"Well, yeah," said Seth. "Twenty six, seven –?"

"Twenty nine foot."

He digested that with another solemn nod of interest. How wide was the Pacific exactly? Ten thousand miles?

"What's it like?" he said, and she got it straight up.

"Like nothing on earth. Literally. You feel the deepest solitude at times. It's meditative. The expanse of sea and sky and horizon seems unchanging, but the crazy thing is, it's constantly changing. The physics of it are astounding. Millions of moments as instant one-offs, again and again and again. The keel, the hull, the mast – they put us right into this endless chaos, creating a nexus point we control. Until we can't. Then we're hers."

"Hers?" said Seth. She laughed, a thrill of wildness in her voice, and he had the odd sensation that this might be the first real adult he'd met in his life.

"Oh yeah, the sea is feminine. Sometimes she's a lady, sometimes she's a bitch, and the bitch chased us into the Coral Sea." She looked around at the bay and smiled. "But this is worth going through that."

Seth felt an unaccountable sense of pride, like he owned the bay or something.

"So, what do you do, Seth?" she said. "A job, a career?"

Seth smiled. You couldn't call what he did a career. As long as there was a chunk of money at the end of it, he'd give it a go. Nothing to be ashamed of.

"I'm security at a place in Cairns. Bands. Rock'n'roll."

"A doorman?"

He nodded, and she made a pleased sound.

"You do look handy," she said. "Kinda rough profession, huh? I imagine around here it'd be a little primitive."

"It's a job, and I'm not so bad at it," he said.

"Do I detect some professional pride there?"

Seth laughed. "Yeah, I 'spose. You do your best, right? It's not like the pub with sweaty blokes coming in straight from work. People are dressed up. Out for a good time."

She grinned softly. "And when you're not working, you come to a place like this and hike around?"

"Well . . . yeah."

"Do you have a hobby or a passion?"

He thought about chicks and cars, guns too, then raised his hands to take in the view.

"This, I suppose. Oh, I like music. Rock music."

Elinore made a sound of admiration, her perfect teeth set in a perfect smile. "You got it all figured out, hey?"

"It's pretty easy," he said, feeling like a small-town boy.

"Have you ever travelled outside of Australia?"

Again, she seemed to be reading him.

"Ah, not yet, but I got some plans for later in the year. Maybe the New Hebrides or Fiji. Indonesia, too."

She made a sound of encouragement. He looked into her eyes for signs that she was just playing him along, but all he saw was a glow of real pleasure, and he resolved that he *would* go overseas.

Maybe it was because she was an American, but he felt something real easy about being with her. She wasn't just a woman, a sexy one at that; she was a possible friend. More than that, he felt a real empathy in her, an intelligent curiosity that wanted to understand what was going on in other people. There was nothing competitive or judgemental about it either, a quality that most blokes didn't have. Though he'd count his father and his mate, Les, as exceptions to that.

Waiting for him to say more, Elinore's smile deepened.

"So, you've travelled a bit, then?" he said, keen to move the conversation away from himself.

With a soft, weary smile, Elinore nodded. "I sure have. Seven thousand miles of it in the last few months. Before that, oh God, I think it was Turkey. It's been a big year."

Seth nodded in interest but felt a sourness inside. He'd spent the year either watching marijuana plants grow, doing his brother's scut work, or pushing around drunks and rooting nurses and office girls in little old Cairns.

"I'm very lucky, though," said Elinore sympathetically. "There's been a lot of 'right place, right time' with me. Sure, I work at being open to the possibilities that come along, but, well . . . I'm not your average American girl."

Seth could believe that.

She looked right at him now, and it was mesmerising. Her big, wide eyes drew him right in, and he had the strongest sensation that she was trying to look right into his head. It was the weirdest bloody feeling, and he had to hide his eyes in the big view.

The Elephant

He helped Jack unload a box of food and cooking gear, a rug, some cushions, and a bag, and they set up camp on the sand under the big beach almonds and matchbox bean trees by the creek mouth.

Jack made coffee on a gas ring using a sealed pot that hissed, the smell bitter and none too appetising. He shook a small jar of white liquid like it was a cocktail shaker.

"Powdered cows, man."

This operation produced three mugs of stuff that looked like watery sump oil. Adding the powdered cows didn't make it look any nicer. In no hurry, Seth put his down to cool. Jack pulled out a pipe and a tobacco tin.

"You want some, man? I got a few pounds of it at Port Vila market. Local stuff."

Seth shook his head. "We grow it here, too," he said.

"Is that a fact?" said Jack, his hands busy with his pipe.

"It's a big industry. Also fishing, cattle, and sugar cane."

"Cows in the tropics?" Jack laughed.

"Mate, in some places the crocs ate the cows, and the farmers had to shoot them."

Jack bellowed with laughter, amazed at what he was hearing. Seth liked that: the bloke's down-to-earthness. With all that hair, he sure looked like a hippie, but there was an edge to him, like he'd grown up tough. He might be on a nice, new yacht, but he was no rich bastard.

Baked beans and eggs were given short shrift.

"Are you kidding, Jack?" said Elinore. "You heard what Seth said. All the fish swimming around here? I'll cook a pilaf with those nangai nuts we got in the New Hebrides – oh, it's so wonderful saying that – and you boys go catch us something succulent to eat."

That sounded great to Seth. Especially how she said succulent. This was cool. He could spend some time with them, ferry them around in the Starcraft, out to the reef even, and with his own rod, they'd all be able to fish.

He gestured to the rocky point on the other side of the creek mouth.

"We'll probably get some flathead there," he said. "We can fish from your inflatable."

"Flathead?"

"Or lizard."

"Lizard? You call a fish a lizard here?"

"You'll see."

"I'm going to just be," said Elinore. She lay back on the rug and made a noise of gratitude. Jack smoked his pipe, then drained his mug. Seth had surreptitiously poured his coffee into the sand after the first mouthful. He'd tried it, and that was enough for a lifetime. How his Italian mates like Sabbo guzzled it down was beyond him.

They went to the yacht in the inflatable, Seth perched on the side, the outboard putting a petrol stink into the air. Approaching the yacht, Seth read – *Vicarious*, San Francisco, on the stern, and he felt a little thrill.

Jack hopped onto the yacht and tied off. Seth put his hands on the rail, keen to see what the cabin of an ocean-going yacht looked like. Jack held up a hand.

"I'll just be a minute, man." He went below.

A little disappointed, Seth looked at the deck, cockpit, and companionway instead. It all looked pretty flash: the beautifully fitted timber deck unmarked and gleaming; the wheel and instrument binnacles shining in the sun.

There were towels and clothes pegged to a line, and on the cabin roof, a cactus plant in a pot and a small carving of an Asian god, that fat, cross-legged fella again. It felt like the plant and statue had been brought up for airing. At the companionway entrance, a toy was affixed: a white plastic rabbit like a good luck charm.

Jack came out of the cabin with a hat on and passed two rods to Seth, then a bucket containing a fish knife and a battered little wooden chopping board.

They puttered a dozen metres away to where the creek mouth curved around the rocky point and anchored over the sandy bottom. Seth got the smaller of the two rods, and they began casting with lures.

Like a good fisherman, Jack didn't talk too much, just a few observations on the world around him, and when he declared that this was a paradise on earth, Seth had to say amen to that.

As he fished, Seth watched the creek at its widest point, where it passed the grove of trees. The water was a deep, cool green. He looked along the edges of the black drifts of decaying vegetation close to the shore, eyes peeled for the flat carapaces of mud crabs.

With a grunt of satisfaction, Jack caught a flathead. Landing it in the inflatable, he held the fish with a piece of greasy cloth to the chopping board and killed it with a knife thrust through the brain.

"I see what you mean," he said. "It's a lizard, alright."

"They taste better than they look," said Seth.

They caught two more, decided that was enough, and Seth directed Jack to take the inflatable up the beach a bit, where they could pull in and clean their catch.

"There's big bloody rats and even bigger lizards around here," said Seth. "Don't want 'em coming around near us."

"Lizards?" Jack held up a fish. "Bigger than these?"

"Oo, yeah. Goannas. Lace monitors. I saw one today above the falls that looked more than two metres long. Half of that's tail, but it was a big one."

"Is that right?" Jack looked suitably impressed.

"You saw the big bird, right? The cassowary?" said Seth. "Well, this is the land that time forgot. Everything's big."

Jack honked with laughter. "Far fucking out. We landed on Skull Island!"

They cleaned the fish, Jack crouching close, all corded brown muscle and smoky beard. Seth showed him how to cut out the cylindrical fillets. Then he picked up the fish frame with its flat gargoyle face.

"Next time we'll use these as mud crab bait," he said. "I brought a trap."

"The mud crabs are big too, right?"

"There's a bit to eat on 'em, that's for sure."

They ate the flathead with Elinore's rice dish and a hot pickle she'd picked up in Fiji. She said succulent again, and Seth, digging her accent, nodded in satisfaction.

She'd got short with Jack when he'd suggested having tinned peas with the fish, and Seth got a glimpse into all that close-quarters living for weeks on end.

After they cleaned up, Seth heard the clink of glass and

an ominous chuckle. Jack, squatting by the food box, held up a bottle of spirits, three tumblers in his other hand.

"You like? It's American bourbon, man."

Seth threw up his hands in surrender. Jack grinned. Elinore wanted to see the view, so they took the bottle and the rug down to the beach. Seth took the lead. Behind him they talked softly but intently for a few moments, and it sounded like something had been decided. Just down from the high-tide line, Seth kicked away a few sticks and laid the rug on the sand. Elinore walked up with three cushions balanced on her head.

"She learnt that at an East Coast finishing school," said Jack. "Or was it in Morocco with your rock star buddies?"

"Don't listen to his bullshit," said Elinore. "I learnt this by just doing it, on beaches all over the planet."

They sat on the rug, and Jack ceremoniously poured two half-full tumblers, then one for Elinore less than a quarter full. They clinked glasses and toasted Zoe Bay. Seth drank, nodded in appreciation. The booze was good.

"It's my first time here, too" he said, and that cued up questions about himself from Jack. He went through it quicker than the other day; again, mostly the truth: his family, Dad a scientist at CSIRO, Cairns, and his place in it, small and easy to describe. When he finished, he took a slug of his drink.

The two Yanks seemed stoked to hear his story, and he sort of understood that. It was a different world to theirs, and seen through the tropical paradise glasses. But what they didn't know was how stifling it got living here.

"So you're a bouncer?" mused Jack. "Lotta tough guys in Cairns?"

"Ahh yeah, a couple."

"Not too many college boys or guys in suits, huh?"

"Nah, not too many."

"You ever lived in Sydney, Seth?" said Elinore.

He shook his head.

"Ever thought about it?"

Seth shrugged. "No plans, but you never know, hey."

Elinore smiled. Jack turned away and spat on the sand.

The bourbon was heaps better than the Suntory, and when Jack poured him a second one, he told Seth there was another bottle in the food box. Taking hold of Seth by the shoulder, he frowned with sincerity.

"You drink as much as you want to, man," he said.

It was a grand thing for him to say, and Seth saw it was just like the man to say it. Jack was a larrikin with a good heart; basically the best sort of bloke you could hope to meet out here. And an American too.

Seth found Americans most interesting – or at least the concept of them interesting, as he'd only met a few briefly while working on doors. But from their music, films, and TV, he had a good idea of what they were like.

He also knew they'd stood by Australia when the Japs had bombed Darwin and invaded New Guinea.

"You know, some Americans died on Hinchinbrook," he said. "In the Second World War."

"On this island?" said Elinore. Seth nodded.

Jack took his pipe from his mouth.

"That figures," he said. "Americans are always dying in a war somewhere."

Seth pointed up at the peaks in the south.

"Behind them is another range. A storm sprung up, and

a bomber flew into Mt. Straloch. Everyone onboard died."

"Oh, that's terrible," said Elinore. "Those poor men."

They sat in silence. Elinore shook her head sadly.

"And still young men get sent off to kill and die," she said. "Angola, Vietnam, Palestine – young lives, possible futures, fed into the death machine."

In his head, Seth heard Sabbath's War Pigs and saw the photos in Time and Newsweek magazines, grainy little black and white windows into conflict and destruction, all happening somewhere else.

Then four years ago, courtesy of the Australian Army, he got his conscription papers, and suddenly somewhere else was knocking on his door.

"I got called up for Vietnam," he said.

"Yeah right, you Australians were there too," said Jack. "Suckers."

Seth frowned. "Hey, hold up, mate. That's a bit bloody steep. You blokes stood by *us* in the war against the Japs."

Jack blew out smoke, his eyes on Seth.

"Yeah . . . we did. Your boys fought hard in Vietnam."

"That's right, they did. A lot of blokes died."

"So, did you see the elephant?"

"See the elephant?" said Seth.

"It's a saying from our civil war," said Elinore. "Young men going off to fight for the first time were going to 'see the elephant.' It's a metaphor for the indescribable, for war in all its confusion and terror."

"So – did you see the elephant?" said Jack.

"Nah," said Seth. He'd been lucky, but there was still a strange part of him that wished he'd gone.

"You hide out from the government?"

"Ah . . . it's a bit of a story."

"I'd say that would be a dead cert with you, man."

Pleased, Seth laughed. "You reckon?"

Jack nodded, took a drag on his pipe. Elinore smiled at Seth and nodded in agreement. It was pretty bloody cool.

"You heard of the Green Berets?" said Jack.

"Sure," said Seth. They were Yank commandos in the Vietnam War, and there was that John Wayne film too.

"Long-range reconnaissance, hit-and-run ambushes, kidnap, interrogation, and demolition," drawled Jack.

Seth now thought of his mate Les, who he'd met at the shooting club last year. He was quiet and unassuming, but a crack shot. They'd become friends, going pig-shooting a few times, and Seth had learnt some real bushcraft from the older man.

Like most blokes who'd been to war, Les didn't really talk about it, but a fella at the club said that he'd been deployed three times in Vietnam, with a good chunk of it patrolling behind enemy lines. Green Beret stuff. It was funny, but Les, slight and polite, didn't look the part at all.

"You ever come across any of them working on doors?" said Jack. "Had to chuck 'em out or keep 'em in line?"

Seth shook his head. Soldiers didn't wear uniforms off duty, and he'd never had problems with a Yank punter. The US Navy had visited Cairns a few times, but the sailors he'd dealt with had been pretty well-behaved.

"I guess you'd have done okay in Vietnam, huh?" said Jack. He gestured at the bush behind them. "You're used to the jungle, living around here."

"Yeah, I 'spose. Except there's no Vietcong," said Seth, saying the word for the first time in his life.

Jack nodded sagely.

"Yeah, true, but you'd have taken out a few of them if ya had to, right?"

"Jack." There was a bite to Elinore's voice.

She smiled at Seth. "Jack's a joker, he loves to play the fool. We went on marches against the war of course."

Seth wondered what that had been like. He'd seen it on TV, the placards and chants, all kinds of people, young and old; the riot police in Europe and the States firing tear gas, the black-clad bastards clubbing people. And there'd been lots of hippies and uni students marching, some real good sorts among them, girls who didn't need bras or make-up.

He'd asked his dad, who had fought in New Guinea against the Japs, what he thought about the protests.

"They certainly have the right to," said Dad, always fair. "Unfortunately, we had no choice in 1941."

Uncle Don, who'd served with Dad, had been adamant about it. "If we don't stop it there, we'll be fighting it here. And from the look of the twits protesting, I sure wouldn't want any of them in charge." Uncle Don was a cop.

"Do you think protest can change things?" said Seth, unaccountably sounding like an interviewer on the ABC.

Jack laughed darkly. It didn't sound bitter, but there was stuff in there that was incomprehensibly big and heavy, and Seth felt the difference in their ages now.

"Yes, I do," said Elinore.

"What about a mass uprising of the people?" said Seth.

"Revolution? Well, yes, I see its agency for change, but what happens afterwards is what really matters. We don't want another Animal Farm, right?"

Seth nodded like he knew what she was talking about.

"See, the real problem people have with revolutions is that you have to fight fire with fire," said Jack. "And to do that you need . . . well, bad men."

"Bad men?" said Seth.

"Yeah. Who do the dirty work. Who break the eggs."

Break the eggs? American was an odd bloody language, thought Seth.

"I disagree," said Elinore, a worn spark in her eyes.

"Sadly it's true, babe," replied Jack. "Uncle Mao said it. Power comes from the barrel of a gun."

Seth had to pay that. He'd seen it happen, fellas getting their way because they had a firearm. Hell, he knew fellas like that. Yep, that Chinese bastard was onto something – without the bang-bang, you were buggered.

Elinore firmly shook her head. Jack's eyes glazed over.

"Violence is no longer a credible answer," she said. "The world is changing fast. With communications, education, and technology, people are waking up and questioning and discarding the status quo. America, Africa –"

"Vietnam," said Seth.

"Exactly. That war has been a high-profile disgrace for the warmongers of the military-industrial complex. The whole world has seen the biggest war machine in history trounced by simple peasants. The imperial age is over."

Outside of a movie set in Roman times, Seth had never heard anyone say anything like that. It sounded amazing.

"You like rock'n'roll, man?" said Jack, gesturing with the bourbon bottle for Seth to hold out his glass.

Elinore's mouth tightened. She looked at the view.

"Yeah, I do," said Seth. He let Jack fill his glass, feeling

Elinore's irritation at the conversation being hijacked.

"What was the last album you bought?" said Jack.

"Me?" It was a cool question to be asked, but Seth didn't know how to pronounce the title.

"Santana. The blue one with the red sun and camels."

"Yeah, he went jazzy with that one. Not his best."

Seth hit his drink. He really liked the album; the songs flying high with a fresh new vibe. So that was jazz?

"I've seen 'em – oh, three times," said Jack.

"True? Santana?"

"Yep. At the Fillmore, too. Before they got big."

"The Fillmore? Where the Allman Brothers double live album was recorded? I've got that album and it's–"

"No, man, that's the Fillmore *East*. In New York. No, let me tell ya about the Fillmore in San Francisco – the original and the best."

And he did, and Seth sat there spellbound, soaking it in. This is more than incredible, he thought. These were the first Americans he'd ever had a yarn with, and *this* is what we're talking about – incredible rock'n'roll stories! Jack had a proper knack for telling them too, and Seth was transported to downtown San Francisco to stand on the street corner as the doors of the auditorium opened and every kind of rock and roll freak poured in.

Jack had seen *Hendrix*. Live in concert. And The Who, and Cream, *and* Jeff Beck. It was unbelievable.

And all the way through his wild stories there was the constant threat of the cops cracking down on people, busting them for being young and dressing differently, for protesting against the bullshit, or for just having a good time. It sounded a lot like far north Queensland.

Jack and Elinore had also marched in demonstrations that had closed down streets. It was what everyone did. And they'd been at huge gatherings, with thousands of groovers listening to top bands all playing for free.

Hearing these tales, Seth felt admiration and envy too. These Yanks had been part of some big things – pretty much history in the making. Would he be able to say the same about himself one day?

Jack began filling his pipe. "Man, I'd dig a smoke of pot. I hoped there'd be some in Suva or Vila, but I sure as hell couldn't find it."

He must really trust me to say that, thought Seth, and the pride he felt gave way to joy that he could oblige Jack. He dug out the smoking tin and chucked it over.

"What –" Jack shot him an 'are-you-for-real' look, then opened the tin. Cackling with delight, he put the tin down and charged on all fours at Seth, headbutting him in the shoulder with a mop of salty hair. Throwing a long arm around Seth, he banged down beside him.

"My man! What a soul comrade you are, the supercargo of weed, the pot port in a storm. My brother, I salute you!"

Laughing hugely, Seth hugged him back. This just got better and better. Over Jack's shoulder, he saw Elinore regarding them with that mystery look on her face.

Jack rolled a joint, and they passed it around. As they smoked, Seth felt a bit anxious. He'd only started growing marijuana in the last two years, and, well, these two were from the epicentre of dope smoking.

When Jack smacked his lips and held his thumb and forefinger up like a French chef, Seth, warmed with pride, almost told them where it came from. But he'd sworn to secrecy, and he took that sort of thing real seriously. He'd certainly tell Robbie and Simon that two cool Americans from San Francisco had thought that their pot was on the money, though.

Nicely stoned, they had another drink.

"So, you got time off work, man?" said Jack.

"Ah, yeah, well, actually I got fired."

Jack raised his eyebrows. Elinore looked at Seth.

"Watcha do? Crack someone's head open?" said Jack.

"No, no, nothing like that." Now he wished he'd kept his trap shut. "Yeah, anyhow, the manager got pissed off, and I got the boot."

"You in a union, right?" said Jack.

Seth shook his head.

"Oh, man. You gotta be in the union to fight them."

"Fight them?" said Seth.

Jack nodded intently. Elinore laughed at him.

"For God's sake, look at you," she said. "Like a wolf with a lamb in front of it."

Seth didn't like that. He was no bumpkin.

"We had a socialist premier in Queensland," he said. "As a young fella, he started a mining union up here."

"Did you say socialist?" Jack looked astounded.

"Mate, we don't live on the moon here," said Seth.

Elinore laughed, her mouth open in delight.

"Red Ted Theodore was his name, and when he stepped down after two terms, people were real sorry to see him go. They won't say that about the prick we got now, but."

"Hell's bells, Jack, my boy," said Elinore. "You look lost for words."

Jack glowered at her.

"We've always voted Labor on Dad's side of the family," explained Seth. "Irish and that."

Jack crowed and raised a fist in triumph.

"I knew it! Felt it when we shook hands, man."

Shaking her head, Elinore laughed at him. Ignoring her, he dished up a brilliant smile for Seth.

"Man, you're not just a cool guy, but you're also part of this grand mission we must all attend."

Awash with bourbon, Seth nodded. He was far from political, but it was nice to be included in a grand mission.

Jack, his aplomb back, started talking about how the man was the strong arm of capitalism, which was the root of all evil, and how capitalism had ruined money for the average man and woman. Seth nodded along, wishing they were talking about bands and the Fillmore again. He'd heard all this before from Dad's mates and from Mr. O'Shea, who'd coached him in boxing.

Elinore watched as Jack talked, her expression between fascination and boredom. Then, finishing her drink, she got up and began collecting driftwood for a fire.

While Jack raved away, Seth watched her, lulled by the simple purpose of her actions and her lithe figure. Jack watched her too as he talked. Then his words came to an end. Seth looked at him, and in the split second before Jack smiled, something primitive moved in his eyes.

Fair enough, thought Seth as he finished his bourbon. Staring at another bloke's missus will get you a hard look anywhere in the world.

He put the tumbler down and stood. Time for a little break. Turning from Elinore and Jack, he began to stroll up the beach.

He heard the murmur of voices, then the scrunch of feet on sand, and Jack came up beside him. When he turned to look, he saw nothing but humorous cheek in the Yank's eyes. Most relieved, Seth grinned back, and they both laughed. What a good bloke, thought Seth. Meeting him, and Elinore, was something that was meant to be.

Jack looked up the beach; Seth followed his gaze. They looked at each other, and it was on – they were going to have a race. They grinned, muscles tensing, and Elinore laughed. She could see what was brewing.

"Whoever gets ahead for three seconds wins," she said.

There was a quick nod of agreement, and they were off, sprinting at breakneck speed. Jack, long legs pumping, kept the pressure on Seth. They went twenty, thirty, forty metres, then Seth began to pull away. To be sure, he counted to five, then quickly decelerated and came to a halt.

Jack thudded past, stopping five metres away. With his back to Seth, he put his hands on his thighs and almost leaned forward as he sucked in air. Sorry, thought Seth. There's just a few too many years on you to outrace me.

With his breath back, Jack picked up a coconut and began tossing it in the air, the fat, brown nut slapping into his palm. Giving Seth a challenging look, he began to jog up the beach, swerving as he went. This display of taking a ball through a field of defenders made Seth laugh, and he quickly ran to join him.

Jack pretended to pass the ball now, and Seth came alongside, hands out for the coconut. But the pass never came. Jack ran on, feigning passes to imaginary players. It didn't seem like they were on the same team.

With a sudden spurt of speed, Jack darted ahead. He'd be scoring a goal up the other end of the beach at this rate, thought Seth. Done running, he came to a halt. Jack threw a look over his shoulder, stopped, and turned. Squaring his shoulders, he broke into a run, zeroing in on Seth in an open invitation to be tackled.

Seth knew a bit about the game Americans played: that they worked out all sorts of manoeuvres beforehand, but that was too brainy, and he just ran at Jack with his arms out. With a benevolent grin, he tackled the Yank nice and solid, but not to smash him into the sand.

But Jack was playing a grand final, it seemed. Ditching the coconut, he threw his shoulder hard into Seth's chest, then grabbed and tripped him. Seth fell on his back, and Jack instantly straddled him, trapping an arm under his knee. Seth tried to buck the bastard off, but he leaned in, pinioning his other arm. Seth gave it one more effort, then gave up and lay still.

Seething with rage, he wanted to kick the Yank's stupid arse. You want to fight me? Then let's drop the bullshit and get properly stuck in!

Jack hopped off, laughing like he'd been playing tag or something. He threw out his arm to pull Seth up. Staring up at the bastard, Seth thought, I'll take your hand, and as I jump to my feet, I'll smash a headbutt into your smug Yank face.

He stuck out his hand and let Jack help pull him to his feet. Brushing off sand, he pushed away his anger and gave Jack a quizzical smile.

"You scared of me, mate?" he said.

Jack, watching him closely, shook his head.

"Listen. Seriously," said Seth. "You two have nothing to worry about from me. Like I said, I'm from Cairns, and everybody knows me there. I'm a good bloke."

His eyes brimming with sincerity, Jack flung his arm around Seth's shoulder. "I know that, man. I know you're a good man. I apologise if I made you sore. I like you; I really do. It wasn't anything personal. It was a test."

"A test? A test for what?" said Seth.

Jack squeezed his shoulder like a coach.

"Let's go see Eli."

Molecules of Light

"What did you do, Jack?" said Elinore as they came up.

"What? What did I do?" said Jack.

"You sat on Seth's chest and wouldn't let him up."

"Ah, it was just a bit of horseplay," said Jack.

Elinore looked at Seth. "Is that right? Or did you want to smack him in the mouth?"

Seth laughed casually, but this was dangerous ground: a woman undermining her man in front of another bloke.

He shook his head. "Nah, it was just horseplay."

Jack nodded in agreement, and for a second, Seth felt like it was his brother Alex standing there.

Elinore watched Seth. He grinned at Jack, who grinned back, and they sat down. Jack poured them both a drink.

"A drink for our efforts," he said, and they toasted each other.

Avoiding Elinore's eyes, Seth looked about. The bay was in complete shadow, and the birdcalls in the forest were changing. The day had turned the corner into afternoon. He thought about going back to the boat. He knew the track now, so it wouldn't take so long. Jack might want to come, and they'd be back here an hour before it got dark.

"You ever had lysergic acid diethylamide?" said Jack.

"Yeah, maybe," said Seth. It kind of rang a bell.

"He means acid," said Elinore. "LSD."

"Oh, yeah. Sure," lied Seth.

Elinore looked like she didn't believe him.

"You handled it okay?" said Jack. "No bad juju?"

"Aww, no more than usual," said Seth, happy to hear them laugh. Well, how was this, he thought. I'm sitting here joking with Americans about taking LSD.

He'd heard the stories, of course: people going bonkers, running around naked in public, jumping out of windows, attacking cops. Apparently some people never came back, ending up in the loony bin for the rest of their lives.

But when he'd actually seen some people who had taken it – two chicks and three blokes at a small party at Clifton Beach – he'd been surprised at how dull it all seemed. In their own world, they sat or lay out on the lawn for hours, sometimes giggling, but with no one doing much at all.

He'd shared his pot, so he didn't need to bullshit Jack and Elinore that he was cool, but people of this calibre didn't often pass through the north, and, well, he wanted to impress them.

"I've had magic mushrooms," he offered.

That was true, and though the hallucinatory rush had been out of this world, he didn't get the 'magic' part. Mushies were rough nuggets, and he'd chucked his guts up both times. Yeah, being queasy, spitting, and wiping away tears wasn't the nicest way to be out of your head.

Beyond the visuals, he wasn't sure if he'd liked the effect much either: everything still vaguely recognisable, like he was far, far gone on rum and pot, with sounds echoing in on themselves and thoughts vanishing the moment they appeared. His skull felt charred the next day.

"Psilocybin, man," said Jack with approval.

"You're a real psychonaut then," said Elinore.

"A psycho – what?" said Seth. "No, no, I'm not going to go nuts or anything."

Elinore laughed. "No, it's not like being crazy. It's like being an astronaut. The psyche is your mind or soul, so a psychonaut travels inside themselves to get into space. Inner space."

It took a few seconds for Seth to get his head around that. It sounded pretty spectacular, but a long way from the nauseous ride of mushrooms.

With a massive grin, Jack clapped his hands together. "So? You wanna take some?"

"Take some?" said Seth.

"Yeah. Lysergic acid diethylamide. LSD. You wanna do some?"

Seth stared, felt his stomach hollow out. Jack laughed.

"Right here, right now. Whadda ya say?"

Well, here you go, thought Seth. Are you ready for this, the big, bad LSD? His bluff had been called, and it looked like it was time to put his psychonaut suit on.

"What better place to take flight than here?" said Jack. "The beauty and the peace? You're halfway there, man."

"Place and people are so important," said Elinore. "Big, rowdy crowds, high-volume noise, alcohol, and violence can fracture a mind. And sleazy bars and heavy clubs can crush a soul. You really need to be in a peaceful place, with like-minded people."

"Eli knows," said Jack. "She was at Millbrook."

It sounded like a university, not that Seth would know.

"The psyche – the high form of the mind – is so open on LSD," she said. "Open to awareness, open to change, and sadly, also open to damage. The greatest disservice we can do with this miracle, this moksha medicine, is to take it at a party or a bar."

"You've done that," said Jack. "We've all done that."

Elinore smiled at Jack, but Seth saw teeth in her eyes.

"Yes, Jack, but we evolve and grow wiser. Nobody needs another acid casualty on the streets. Even if you don't fall that far, that unfocused hedonism is a terrible waste of a chance – a very real chance to step out of a damaged or programmed self. It's not about getting high – it's about getting outside of yourself and *really* moving up."

She laughed in sudden delight, gestured at everything around them with her hands.

"Of course! Have you read Island?" she said to Seth.

"Read Island?" His brain groped for comprehension.

"Yes, the book."

"Yeah, yeah," said Jack with a dismissive wave of his hand. "It doesn't matter, man, because when you get right down to it there's nothing like actual experience. Right?"

He reached out, bringing up his forefinger.

"What?" said Seth.

Jack nodded at his fingertip – at the minute square of white paper perched there.

"That's it?" Seth was scared it was going to blow away.

"Blotter," said Elinore. "Very clean, fairly strong. From our hometown. Made by alchemists. Now, that's a full-size dose. You going to be okay with that?"

With a lurch of anxiety, Seth nodded confidently.

"You gotta knock it back with bourbon, man. Like a real American," said Jack.

Seth laughed. The Yank was a picture: bearded, wild-eyed, and smiling like a pirate Santa.

"Lick your finger and pick it up," directed Jack.

Seth wet the tip of his finger, picked up the tiny square of paper, and held it up to his eyes. Really? There wasn't much of it.

Jack now held up his own white scrap of paper. He put his finger in his mouth, then took a swig from his tumbler.

"Well, there you go," he said. "Countdown to ecstasy."

Seth looked at his fingertip.

"If you don't want to, that's okay," said Elinore.

"But you'll regret it for the rest of your life," said Jack.

Seth laughed nervously.

"You remember the very first time you got stoned?" said Jack. "And how you couldn't believe this shit had been out there all along and you didn't know about it?"

Seth nodded. He did.

"Well, it's a hundred times that feeling with LSD."

"Sounds good," said Seth, and he licked the paper off his finger and chased it down with bourbon.

Jack put an imaginary horn to his mouth and sounded off a fanfare. "You are now officially an American," he proclaimed. "God bless your acid-spangled soul."

Seth looked at Elinore.

"I'm not having any," she said. "It's best that one of us stays straight. To make coffee."

"We got ourselves a chaperone," said Jack. "She'll keep us in line."

"And this place is so beautiful. I want to feel it straight," said Elinore. "I'm just digging being on dry land."

That prompted silence, and they sat sipping bourbon and looking at the view.

"Mind if I roll another joint?" said Jack. "To ease us in."

"Mate, go for it," said Seth.

Jack rolled up, and as they smoked, a kind of reverence fell over them. They'd all made it to Zoe Bay, and it was as big and wild and beautiful as they'd expected.

On the horizon, a boat cleared the southern headland, its outrigger frames sticking up into the air.

"What's that?" said Jack. "A fishing boat?"

"Yep," said Seth. "A trawler. From Innisfail, maybe.

"Likely to come in here? Anchor for the night?"

Seth shook his head. "Nah, there'd have to be a pretty bad storm for that to happen."

"Okay," said Elinore slowly. Jack nodded reflectively, and they both sat lost in thought.

Well, good for them, thought Seth. It was their first proper sit-down and relax in, what, nine days. And with a smoke and a drink too. They were soaking it up.

Suddenly restless, he stood and went down to the water, where he watched little waves break across the sand. When would the LSD come on? Maybe it wouldn't work after its long journey across the Pacific. He stared at the foam circling his feet and toes, alert for optical illusions. The waves washed in, washed out, but nothing changed.

He turned and looked up at the glorious amphitheatre of the range, and – Jesus! – shock rocked him. The peaks and scarps up there were glowing with impossibly clear light. Every little detail was alive. But how in hell could rock be alive? But he could see it clearly. It was as if his eyes had been dirty and were now wiped clean.

He looked around. Wow. With thrilling wonder he saw glowing platinum clouds vibrating against a buzzing blue sky. In the sea, millions of gemstone facets of aquamarine and emerald sparked. Between the headlands of the bay, the horizon now hovered in *front* of the sky and sea, and the air itself was visible, moving around him in currents.

He quickly went back up the beach and sat down.

"What's happening?" said Elinore. "You cool?"

"Yep, it's happening," said Seth. "I'm just gonna sit here and get my head around it."

Elinore laughed. "You won't be doing that."

Seth tried to smile, but overwhelming sensation burst through him, the force of its rush like a river in instant flood. He lay back, and the sand vanished under him.

"See you on the other side," said Elinore.

He made to reply, but his lips wouldn't move, and the LSD rolled in – irresistible, expansive, majestic, clear – and the absolute fucking *isness* of it was astounding. This wasn't mucking around. This was where it was at.

Anything of who he was, or thought he was, was gone. Within and without, he was flummoxed. This was beyond imagining. With his brain wide open, all rational concepts blew away as the world in its named, ordered, and thought-out form disappeared. In its place was everything happening.

Now all was all, and he knew what gave the truth its meaning. He wasn't the mind in the body of a man on a beach on an island anymore – he was molecules of light. On an endless wave, the drug carried him aloft.

With all thought and emotion now superfluous, a magnificent profundity rang through him as he felt an utterly new way of being. He wasn't here; he was *of* here, sharing existence at an atomic level, seeing and being infinite things. He had become everything.

An eon passed in this state of being: undetailed, untold, unknown. He knew it was happening to him, but that was all. Things like existence and cognisance were arbitrary, relative, and light and sound and the breeze on his skin became interchangeable. The perceivable phenomena of the world receded into a deep buzz, eyes closed or not.

Then he felt an infinite emptiness where nothing could exist. This awful vacuum was unanswerable, irrefutable, and crushing in its totality. He felt a grand mal shock, an existential death, as he experienced this complete void.

Losing his identity and all rational thought was insanity enough, but if this utter nothingness swallowed him now – he'd never come back. Scared for his soul, he struggled, his arms and legs moving in the sand.

Then massive subsonic horns sounded, a visceral blare that blasted through his body, and he felt an awareness existing outside of himself: a deep presence he knew had always been there but had somehow never noticed.

Awake and sentient, it was like him – but it didn't need him. Distant, cool, unattached, it radiated pure calm. As he took this presence in, the void receded, leaving in its place another kind of nothingness that hummed with tranquillity like the thoughts of stone or water.

The sentience moved on, and he was reborn, trembling in the mad glory of the physical world. Waves hissed and roared, and he smelt the fecundity of trees and flowers. He was back in the Garden, the spirit of place cradling him, his skull open in wonder – and he felt a miracle.

It exploded through him in gorgeous simplicity. He was in the holy instant, and he could see how it was all there ever was and had ever been, only happening in the now, and far beyond meaning or intent. This instant was the real thing; everything else inherently an afterthought.

The unadulterated perfection made him swoon. Blown away by its wonder, he now saw existences and infinities between increments of time, micro-sliced moments filled with every thought and sensation imaginable. Zapped by this power, he soared up on a psychic thermal and knew a glorious peace. He was here; he was home.

Time, neither static nor moving, madly throbbed in a stasis where it existed and didn't exist, and in the midst of this phenomenon, he felt inspired to sit up, and it was easy. Letting the action take him, he stood and stretched out his arms and felt shivers of delight. Air bounced off his skin and face, and he watched what his eyes were seeing: a cavalcade of colours and movement.

From beside him came a lovely feminine laugh, and he opened or turned his eyes on. There was an angel looking at him, but an angel you could touch and kiss. He knew who she was, but he couldn't name her.

He laughed back, and it came out as a gurgle. Now she was close, glowing with wisdom and care, the smell of her incredible. In dumb sensation he felt her take his hand in hers and gently squeeze.

"You okay?"

He made a happy noise.

"I'm watching you," she said.

He nodded, so very grateful she was here. Vibrating in chemical bliss, he sighed with pleasure. They stood side-by-side, her arm around his waist, her breast warm against his arm, and he never knew two people could be this close. Her energy flowed into him. Then her eyes held his, and he felt her right there in his head with him. Or were they both together outside of their heads?

In completely unfiltered communication, he *knew* her, her vast intelligence and hard-driving force, her many accomplishments, and the certainty with which she made things happen. But her power had an edge, a ruthlessness, and he saw her impatience – and fear too.

In her eyes, or in his head, he now saw an offer, an offer from her that included everything if he wanted to go that far. She needed him, wanted him too, but it would be all or nothing. It meant crossing a line.

She laughed, her eyes challenging him. She knew what he'd seen. "Will you help me?"

He stared, not sure if she'd spoken or if he'd imagined it. She waited, the dark pools of her eyes consuming him.

If he could think, he wouldn't know what to think, so he closed his eyes and listened to the hum. On the screen of his mind, patterns formed, dissolved, and formed again.

Then he was walking along the beach, or maybe floating on a shoreless sea of wonder, and from the sky came a cry, some creature passing, and on an instant physical whim, he made to fly, leaping up into the air. He did this until he didn't, then he sat on the sand and felt the holy instant re-embrace him. From the tips of his toes to the top of his scalp, he buzzed with an endless electric glee.

Now he saw movement – a figure dancing against an indigo sky. A woman moving on long, supple legs, breasts bare. With the world frameless, he saw her with complete lucidity: lissome, elemental, sexual, a goddess dancing in the dusk. She moved boldly, carving out the air around her, and he wanted to touch her without hands or fingers.

Humming like a dynamo, he watched her until the light left the sky and night blanketed the beach. Stars picked out the horizon and headlands, and in the darkness, sets of chemical waves rolled through him, organic patterns and bird-like shapes riding them in.

Then a spark, an incredible yellow. Flames flared and crackled. A woman crouched there, face intent, her hands feeding a fire. It was a primeval rebirth, and he felt deep, perennial comfort. The fire's dancing light was a swarm of golden butterflies. He fluttered with them, suspended between destruction and creation, and, like a moth, he moved closer to the flames.

A man was sitting by the fire, someone he knew. With a grunt of greeting, he sat down next to him. Shoulder-to-shoulder they felt as solid as blocks of wood. The woman handed him a cup, told him to drink. As he did, he saw it was Elinore, and he felt so very glad he'd met her and that she was here. They sat watching the butterflies for a while, and he saw that it was Jack sitting next to him, and he smiled uncontrollably at this wonderful man.

Elinore stoked the fire. She looked feral, with glittering dingo eyes, her strong bare thighs burnished by firelight. Seth felt something bigger than desire for her. It was full of sex, but not really of it, and he touched her body in his mind without guilt or shame that Jack was there.

In the swell and fall of the LSD, he remembered sitting with her, her arm around him, her eyes going right into him – and a psychic uppercut floored him. He knew her; he'd always known her. She was every woman he'd ever cared for and loved, but his heart broke as he realised she might be the only woman he'd ever feel this with.

Then he saw it wasn't love, and it wasn't her. It was the understanding that love was a paradox and a mystery that he could burn down the rest of his life looking for an answer to. He'd suffer doing that, and every woman he got with would suffer too. To stay sane, he had to live with the unknowable and just make the best love he could.

Another realisation stunned him, then another, and all he could do was smile at this parade of enlightenment. It was endless; it was always.

The fire billowed with warm colours, its energy a bright sanctuary. The night was thick, dark velvet around him, the wood smoke something that the very first people had smelt, and this sense of the continuum was so strong he knew that he'd lived forever and would live forever.

He noticed a pair of feet on the rug, and he stared at the pale, bodiless things until he saw it was Elinore asleep in a blanket. He needed a pee, and he got up and walked away from the fire, the dried crust of the sand crunching under his feet.

Away from the light, the stars were breathing with the ebb and flow of galaxies, and he heard the fading hiss of small waves in the bay breaking all the way up the beach. Taking a pee on LSD was amazing, and he stood there for the longest time shivering with sensation.

Back at the fire, he felt things changing; thoughts and ideas emerging like animals after a bush fire, and he sat in a wonderfully alive silence with Jack, both staring at the flames. They were closer than any talk could bring them, and besides, there was nothing that needed saying.

He could feel that Jack had lived a tough life, that he'd done heavy things. But so had he, and that was an outlaw bond that no straight bastard could ever understand. And this, taking acid with someone, made that same kind of secret bond. If you didn't know – you didn't know.

Jack poured them a bourbon. Seth rolled a joint and lit it up, and they sat wordlessly drinking and smoking like old mates who had shared a lifetime of stuff together. But their silence buzzed with import and possibility, each moment more amazing than the next. It's crazy, thought Seth; this drug makes doing nothing feel monumental.

Now a semblance of reality began to return, and he and Jack began talking, softly and slowly, about nothing much in particular. The words didn't seem so important. What mattered was the rapport they'd forged over the last few hours. The affinity they'd first felt drinking, smoking, and talking about rock music had deepened into something much more profound. Seth hadn't just made a new mate; he'd found a brother.

They grew louder, quietly guffawing at nonsense. Then they both looked at Elinore sleeping, and they got up and wandered up the starlit beach. In a low growl Jack began speaking of a tropical paradise, an island far beyond the machinations of man, where the moksha medicine healed the mind and soothed the soul.

Seth listened, and he knew that this island was real and that he'd done the right thing in coming here to it. His anger at his brother's manipulations and his frustration at the small-mindedness of Cairns had vanished. He was better than all that; he was above it. The LSD and the island, and these two amazing people had cleared all the rubbish away.

Jack came to a halt. "What's that?"

Seth stopped, and they listened, the stars peeping down at them. From the tree line came the crackle and crack of twigs and leaves being stepped on – the sound of someone coming through the forest towards the beach.

"It's him," Jack whispered, and the fear in his voice sent huge unease through Seth. Him? He remembered Jack's raised hand barring him from boarding the yacht. Had there been someone else onboard?

The rustling and snapping stopped as footsteps came out onto the sand. Whoever it was wasn't shy.

"Oh, no. Shit, no," whispered Jack.

Seth felt for the lighter in his pocket.

In the darkness, Jack grabbed his arm. "Will you help us? Please, man. Please."

His voice was a panicked gibber. Seth hated it.

In a swish, swish, swish of sand, someone came up to them and stopped. Neither man breathed. Seth pulled his Zippo out, held it up, and flicked it lit.

At eye level, a big, blue dinosaur face stared at them.

"Oh, shit," croaked Jack.

"Don't move," said Seth, and he let the flame go out.

"Okay, mate, just turn around, and we'll slowly walk back to the fire." He turned, reached for Jack.

"Fuuuck," whispered Jack, and he turned too.

"Here we go," crooned Seth, "Nice and slow."

He began walking, his hand tight on Jack's arm. As they approached the fire, Jack's voice began rising in a quaver of terrified glee. "Fuuuuuck, man. Fuuuuuccck."

At the fire they turned and looked back. Jack's face was filled with wild joy. Whoever he'd thought was out there wasn't a patch on being bailed up by a cassowary.

Big liquid eyes glinted with firelight a few metres away. They all watched each other for a minute, then soft thuds sounded on the sand as the big bird wandered off.

Jack grabbed Seth and hugged him.

"Man," he said. "Thank you. Oh man, this place."

Seth hugged him back, loving the bloke.

Quietly giggling, they sat by the fire again. Jack found his tobacco, and as he filled the pipe, his grin faded and his face grew still. It looked like a wax mask now, with the hair of his beard sewn into yellowed skin. He looked dead.

Feeling jangled by this, Seth looked away. The purity of the trip was gone now. Something had ended. Staring at the fire, Jack smoked. Pushing away unease, Seth lay back on the cool sand and closed his eyes.

Strange hallucinations played across the inside of his eyelids: great expanses of intricately sharp volcanic rock; thousands of nocturnal herd animals looking up at the edge of a spotlight's sweep; a rash of blisters or spots of mould on skin, or was it rock? It all began to merge, and he drifted into a half sleep.

Sometime later he surfaced from this limbo, his mind now thankfully clear of the weirdness. He sat up and saw the first light in the sky. Jack was snoring. Next to him, wrapped up like a mummy, Elinore lay sleeping.

Dawn began to break over the Coral Sea. Squadrons of clouds sailed across the sky. The sea danced with light. It was wonderful seeing daybreak, and the light, colour, and movement seemed to bring the acid back. He sat there for a while, feeling hollowed out but somehow wonderfully solid too. He heard a contented sigh next to him.

"Just like the song, hey?" said Jack.

They smiled at each other. Seth found his canteen and drank deeply. He looked at Elinore sleeping, turned back, and saw Jack watching him.

"She's tired, man," he said.

Seth nodded. "Up most of the night. Like Mother Hen."

"That storm really took it out of her. Can't say I was too happy either. I could see 'lost at sea' being carved into tombstones back in San Francisco," said Jack.

His gaze went back to Elinore. "She's on solid ground now. She'll sleep all day."

Seth nodded in sympathy, and they watched the dawn. After a while, flights of birds came across the water into the bay. They grew closer, then flew into the forest further up the beach. More appeared on the horizon.

"Pigeons," said Seth. "Really good to eat."

"Is that right?" Jack grinned like he could taste them.

"Yeah. But there's no killing doves here."

"There's no killing doves here. Man, you're a poet, too."

Unsure, Seth laughed. It was an odd thing to say.

"Where are they going?" said Jack.

"There are fruit trees in off the beach."

Jack stared at him, then in unspoken synchronicity they got up and started walking. When they got to where the birds were passing overhead, the flap of wings audible in the still air, they went into the forest, and Seth began looking for the fruit trees.

Stepping around their flat buttress roots, they stopped under a couple of big quandong trees. Seth pointed to the bright blue fruit lying on the ground. Above them came the drawn-out, almost human cries of the unseen birds – *'bollocks are blue, bollocks are blue.'*

"They're wompoo pigeons," said Seth.

"Wompoo?" Jack listened carefully. "Okay, I get it. They're saying it – whollic-pa-boo, whollic wom-poo."

"No, they're saying something else."

Jack cocked his head and listened again.

"Bollocks are blue," said Seth.

Jack listened some more, then nodded.

"Okay. Bollocks. You mean balls, right?"

Seth nodded, happy to see the American copping some linguistic confusion for a change. Jack laughed.

"Yep, I can see an Aussie guy alone in the jungle coming up with that."

No Whys or Hows

Sitting on the beach, with Jack and Elinore now asleep at the camp under the grove of trees, Seth felt like he was home. Three people and a yacht on a faraway beach. This was how life should be – going to top places, meeting cool people, and taking incredible drugs with them.

It wasn't just the LSD buzzing inside making him feel this. It was also these two way-out-there Americans who'd come out of the Coral Sea, real adventurers who crossed oceans and lived a rock'n'roll life to the full. Psychonauts.

He had imagined there were people like this, so it was bloody fantastic to see that they really existed. They were proof of another way, another world, and this validated a whole lot of stuff he'd thought about and hoped might be.

Living beyond society's boundaries, doing just what you wanted, like it was your right to do so. It was inspiring. He wasn't about to sail across the Pacific or march in the streets just yet, but he'd had a taste of the possible, and he liked it.

He went into the camp and gazed at them: heads on cushions, bodies turned from each other, and Elinore's shorts rucked up, baring the curve of her bum cheeks. In a zap of lust, he remembered her dancing last night, her sweet bare breasts, her long smooth legs. She seemed the ideal woman – clever, sexy, confident, and worldly, with a vibe and energy he'd love to taste, even just once.

He reined it in, quietly got his rucksack, and went back onto the beach. Squatting down just beyond the high tide line, he dug his hat and the Aerogard out. He put on the long-sleeved shirt and his boots, then hung the rucksack in a tree so they'd know he hadn't taken off for good.

It was a beautiful day, and he didn't want to waste a second of how he was feeling right now. He'd take a stroll up the track, and in the magic of the forest he might see more wompoos, or even the cassowary again. And when Jack and Elinore woke up, he'd go get the boat and cook them up a bonza breakfast.

In amongst the trees it was a cool, crisp green. Little waves of the LSD caressed him as he walked, and he remembered a dream he used to have as a kid: camping in the bush, inexplicably alone, he'd get this mad urge and run away from his camp. Then he'd sleep in the dirt like a beast, drink water from creeks, and hunt prey with his hands and teeth. It was raw and animalistic, and he would wake up feeling strangely liberated.

Time gently unspooled as he walked. At the swampy creek he saw something move. Creeping over, he spied a big heron picking its way through the mangrove roots. He watched it hunt, checking out the grey plumage and intent white face. Entranced, he passed an age with the bird.

Back on the track, he sauntered along until he saw the melaleuca swamp coming up. Not fancying wet boots, he left the track and followed a small gully going south.

Sunshine pooled on boulders, and vines hung in loops off trees. He smelt sap and saw birds flit overhead. Bright orchids hung from rocks. It was a whole world in here, an *ecosystem* as Dad would say. The gully began rising, going up alongside a ridge, and he realised he was behind the little range of hills he'd taken a look at yesterday. Pleased at this serendipity, and now enjoying a sense of purpose, he slipped his sunglasses on and began looking for a cave or a possible campsite again.

The gully was dusty and dry, with skinks zipping off as his shadow moved across granite boulders. Above him on the ridge he saw slabs of exposed rock, weathered brown and grey. From the trees ahead came the cackling chatter of friarbirds. He climbed up and saw them darting about in a four-metre-high banksia tree. In its branches, flowers floated strangely, looking for all the world like gas flames.

Intrigued, he made for the banksia. With angry cries, the friarbirds challenged him. As he came up, they flew off in a rage. He examined one of the cylindrical flowers. In an optical trick, the hundreds of spikes attached to the soft core seemed to glow with an inner light, the colours a deep red surrounded by mauve, grey, and blue. What a marvellous thing to see, real and not some hallucination.

He moved on. It was growing warmer, and when he saw a shady grove of trees, he went and sat in their shade. Twinkles and buzzes of druggy pleasure moved through him. Feeling most mellow, he pondered the LSD trip.

Relinquishing his personality and all comprehension had been a thrill he'd liked. Losing your mind actually worked with this stuff. It was like his brain had given over the wheel to him, and without its constant chattering, he had time to see and feel the world as it truly was. A part of him now felt obsolete.

But he'd been so vulnerable when it came on. Like a baby, he'd been utterly defenceless, and that went right against the grain with him. Yep, he'd be on his guard next time. He'd know what to expect.

And that void. Seeing the world existing without him had been a huge shock. The absolute nothingness it had made of him was terrifying. But he hadn't fallen in. He'd looked at it, and he'd come back. He'd seen the elephant.

Coming off the acid was nice, nothing like the edgy grittiness of mushrooms. Lying back on a flat rock, he watched the wind move the canopy and listened to the murmur of the leaves, and that sense of being home enfolded him.

With a start, he awoke. He'd drifted off, cradled in the bosom of a green and brown goddess. It was a wonderful feeling, and he could easily go back to it, but he sat up and felt a deep truth – he was bloody starving. He checked his watch. Jesus, he'd slept for three hours. Elinore and Jack must be awake by now, and they'd be hungry too. All the food on the boat began scrolling through his head like a menu, and his stomach started piping a marching tune.

Energised, he made his way back down the gully, deftly hopping and jumping in a continuous flow of movement. On the flat, insects buzzed in the trees as he hurried back to the beach. With food on his mind, it seemed to take forever, the forest now twice the size it had been.

Coming out onto the beach, he saw with surprise, then curious anticipation, that there was now an orange-hulled yacht anchored next to *Vicarious*. And not very far from him someone was coming – a bare-chested, clean-shaven bloke walking in very close to the tree line.

Seth watched him appear and disappear through the foliage, then come into view. He was barefoot, wearing faded shorts, and when he saw Seth, he exploded into a run. Rocketing in, no expression on his face, the man was tanned, short-haired, athlete fit, and holding something half-hidden against his thigh – a bush knife.

Wild energy spiked through Seth, his perception going into overdrive. Maybe it was the LSD, or that he'd always been quick with violence, but he instantly spun around and bolted up the track.

In an instant – two, maybe three seconds – he'd seen that this man meant murder. His speed, the hard, vacant face, the hidden blade – the bastard was out to kill him!

On a bullet of adrenaline, Seth's feet scarcely touched the ground. The forest accelerated past in a grey-green blur. There were no whys or hows about it, just the simple animal urge to survive. If he'd ever run hard in his life – all the footy games and escapes from blokes keen to give him a flogging – then now was the time to pour it on.

The track unfolded before him. He flowed through the air like he was on a Yamaha 250, its throttle all the way back. Time vanished. He felt in front of himself, his mind ahead of his feet. Flowing around curves, his reflexes spun on new gears. He didn't need to look or think. Outside of his head, he could see the way ahead.

Then water exploded over his ankles, up his shins, and melaleuca and pink bloodwood joined overhead. He was in the swamp, and over the noise he was making came percussive splashes not far behind him. It sounded like a big, trained dog was closing in.

The melaleuca swamp was an obstacle course of roots, submerged branches, and slippery tussocks of grass, and he stayed alert for a foot to go down a hole at any moment.

The mossy green bulk of a log appeared; its length and width meant a runaround he didn't have time for. On the top of the log, he saw the stump of a branch, and he ran at it. Sailing in, he dropped his water canteen, leapt up onto the log, and grabbed the stump to pull himself up. As he slid over the log, it broke, and he splashed down hard on the other side, his boots throwing water up onto his mouth. Wiping it off, he spat hard and took a good, sharp look at what lay ahead. Then, calf-deep, he charged on.

A tree line was emerging: the swamp's edge. Looking as he ran, he saw it – a vertical patch of darkness, the gap between two straight tree trunks side-by-side: the spot he'd marked yesterday. He made a beeline for it.

He rushed past the trees, his boots now hitting solid ground with a machine thump, thump, thump. Leaves, fronds, batted at his face, and his vision blurred for mad seconds as a spiderweb tore off on his face. He clawed it away, went headfirst through some elephant's ear, a spray of tiny fallen flowers coming off the massive green leaves.

The forest was shoulder close, but he could see the track at his feet: a faint vertical slot through the green, a pale line on the deep brown earth. The bush grew darker and thicker. He was in jungle now, and his head, shoulders, and arms jerked and jumped automatically, dodging coils and loops of wait-a-while cane, their endless rows of clothes-snagging hooks flashing by.

Startled pigeons exploded overhead, wings smacking against leaves. Something squeaked in alarm as it bolted away through the undergrowth. Seth's boots relentlessly pounded the ground.

Palms now appeared, quickly forming up great walls of

trunks. Dead fronds crackled underfoot. He ran on and on, the very act of it a kind of fuel. But when he came out of the palm forest, still going at atomic speed, he knew he couldn't maintain this gut's effort pace much longer. He'd run too far at too high a speed.

The crazy man chasing him must have slowed down getting around the log back in the swamp, and when Seth hit a straight bit of the track, he flashed a look back over his shoulder. It was like a horror movie – the bastard was metres away, expressionless, running hard.

Now awful dread filled Seth. If he didn't change this situation right now, he was going to die, hacked down in a welter of blood, his shouts unheard, his life suddenly over. It seemed impossible, but it was about to happen.

Seeing the dark bulk of liana-hung trees rising up on a slope, he left the track and ran towards them. He saw a steep ridge, the vine-encrusted trees leading to it. Head down, protecting his eyes, he dodged and ducked into a great web of branches and trunks, all woven together with vines, creepers, and fat lianas.

Everything was close, eager to snag, so he slowed and found a different way to move as fast as he could. It wasn't easy travelling in here, but the confined space would hamper the swing of the bush knife. And there might be rocks near the slopes of the ridge he could fill his pockets with. When he left the vine thicket, he'd wait in ambush – then peg them right into the evil bastard's head.

Leaping through the lianas on the ground and hanging from trees, he looked out for potential traps. The big and little vines made webs and nets, and with logs and tree trunks thrown in, there'd be places he wouldn't be able to get through. Run into the wrong tangle of vegetation, and he'd be in a living cage that the murder man would cut him down in.

He made a desperate racket smashing through, banging into liana ropes running up into the canopy, and crashing through vertical sails of creepers dark with fallen leaves and branches. Shaken loose by his flight, vegetative debris fell through beams of light: dried, powdery bark; bits of twigs; crumbs of thorns, leaves, and stalks – a gritty, blinding jungle dust that he needed to avert his eyes from.

A crackle of feet in the leaves came from behind him, then the thud of feet. Seth skidded on vines, branches, and rotting leaves, his thighs and calves working hard. He heard the bush knife thunk into a vine. Then again. He flashed a look, saw Murderman swarming in, jumping, twisting, and squeezing sideways to get at him. Staggered by this lethal one-mindedness, Seth went even faster.

He plunged deeper into the thicket, crab-scrabbling around tree trunks in the musty twilight. The ground was uneven, the start of the ridge. He bashed through, vines corkscrewed all about him, and, damn it, slipped.

He slid back a metre, his boots scrabbling on dirt. He saw the vines jumping with jungle dust as a figure crashed out into a shaft of sunlight right by him. Murderman's sweat-bright face was covered in leaf fragments, a spiked curl of dried lawyer-cane in his buzz-cut hair; his eyes blank, more reptile than ape. He was an appalling force of nature that only death could tame.

In this micro-sliver of time, Seth saw that the bastard was holding his Machet 15! And there was a tattoo on his bicep: a globe on an anchor with an eagle on top.

A knot of lianas separated them, and Murderman began quickly jabbing at Seth with the Machet, the steel tongue flashing between coils of vine. Seth twisted like a go-go dancer in a cage as the blade probed for flesh and sinew.

Their deadly dance knocked vines, bringing down a blinding fall of jungle dust. Seth, forced to look down, saw a bare foot. Lunging sideways, he stamped hard on it, and the bastard fell back with a hoot of pain. Seth turned, tore up the slope, bouncing off trunks and vines, his boots tearing through the thick leaf litter.

Bursting out of the thicket, he saw boulders, then a small cliff that he veered away from. Ascending quickly, he tried to use bushes and shrubs as cover without losing speed. He got to the top of the ridge and ran through a line of eroded granite outcrops into the forest. His lungs burned, he couldn't feel his legs, but he kept running.

After a few minutes he stopped and listened over his mad breathing to distant birdsong. He sucked in air, his chest heaving, his eyes roaming the ground for rocks of a good size to carry and throw. With the hair standing up on his neck, he let long seconds trickle past until he felt sure the crazy man wasn't right up his arse anymore.

But Murderman was coming – he knew it. The bastard wasn't human; he was a machine. Seth shivered. This was like a nightmare, but it was stone-cold real.

With dread keening through him, he began to run again, slower now, and after five minutes, he stopped and pricked up his ears. The forest was still, and he sat down for a moment and tried to think.

Befuddled, rattled, stunned. It didn't do it justice. He tried to get his mind to work. Then it hit him – he couldn't go to the boat just yet. If he led the bastard to it, he might not get off the island alive. He needed to go higher up and lay low for a few hours. He checked his watch and saw it was already pushing midday.

It took a real effort to concentrate, but he closed his eyes and visualised what he had to do. Avoiding most of the track, he'd get to Nina Beach in the late afternoon, then he'd use the shadows to get close to the boat. He'd stay hidden as night fell, then get it out onto the water in the darkness.

With a plan made, it now slammed him over the head. Elinore and Jack! His guts turned to ice. If Murderman had hunted him so relentlessly, what chance did those two have? And it was odds on the evil bastard had come here with evil mates. Bestial images of degradation and death pierced his mind. He felt a stunning wave of despair.

He loudly said, "That's enough," and it seemed to work. He said it again, then once more, and with his lid on tight, he began moving through the trees.

It was good having a plan and even better keeping your cool, but damn it if he didn't look back over his shoulder more than a few times.

After an hour of bush-bashing, something long and pale came into view, and he soon saw a stretch of sunlit rocks going steeply up a valley, and disappearing into the forest. Many metres across, it had to be one of the creeks that fed the lagoon down in Zoe Bay.

But unlike the creek he'd crossed yesterday, there was no water in this one, a real pity as he was as thirsty as a runaway dog. Coming out of the trees, he felt very exposed in the glare of the dry watercourse.

Crossing it was deceptive; gravity both friend and foe. Leaping from rock to rock was no-false-move stuff. He couldn't risk a broken ankle or leg. If the killer G.I. Joe didn't find him, the goannas would, and they didn't stand on ceremony waiting for you to die.

He took a knock on an elbow sliding down a boulder, barked a shin, and his boots saved his feet a few times, wedging hard into rock crevices, the leather crushing in around his heels and toes. Avoiding boulders and jammed logs, he angled upwards across the creek bed.

It was sweet relief to hit cool shadow again. Hopping off a big rock back into the trees, he began following the creek bed up, moving through myrtle trees covered in tiny white flowers. Eventually he turned away from the creek and went into a valley, its far end full of trees of considerable size. Rock seams began poking up, basalt outcrops clogged with epiphytes and shrubs.

This was death adder country, and he kept alert, ready to leap aside at any second. Gaps in the canopy gave him glimpses of the peaks above him, the exposed rock going up hundreds of metres. The valley walls steepened, grew closer, and he went in under blackbeans and bloodwoods of stupendous girth, their branches all grown together like arms around shoulders, the great bases of the trees deep with fallen vegetation. This forest detritus had piled up over time, hiding big, fat roots and gnarly knobs, and he nearly fell a few times.

An area of light now materialised in the forest, growing longer and longer as he approached. It was the bottom of a cliff, lit by sunlight streaming through the gap between the rock and the trees. The ground along its base was clear and he went into the light and squinted up. Disappearing into the blue, the cliff didn't look like it had an end.

Slipping between trees and rock, he easily followed the cliff, but after a few hundred metres it began bulging with protrusions, rockfalls, and boulders. Clambering around these obstructions, he saw a small cave mouth at roughly head height. Slowing to look, he smelt a rank, ammonia-like odour: the accrued excrement of many animals.

Stepping past the stink, he saw right by his face, a snake coiled on a branch, watching him with one golden eye, its tongue probing the air: a little python waiting for dusk and for bats to emerge from the cave.

Seth had a visceral flash of all the animals getting eaten on the island right now: grabbed, crunched, gulped down; hundreds of creatures hunting, killing, and dying. And here he was right with them, in the jungle on the side of a mountain on an island in the middle of nowhere.

He hit loose rock, lots of unseen ankle rollers underfoot and went back into the trees. Skirting the rocky, jumbled cliff, he made for a spur of ground rising up through the forest. He needed to get above the trees so he could get a proper look at where he was going. And see who was coming.

Going up the spur, he grabbed saplings and bushes to help boost his ascent. It was heavy going, but it wasn't too far now, the canopy thinning fast, the sunlit open ground just metres away. Coming through the tree line, he began to flag. Out on the open ground, a curving, wind-blown slope of grass and sedge, he walked for a few more metres, then sank to the ground. Catching his breath, he looked around, blinking in the hot brilliance of the sun.

Hundreds of metres up the side of the big valley behind Zoe Bay, he'd come out right under the great peaks of Mt. Bowen and The Thumb. The view was huge up here: wisps of cloud threw shadows across acres of rock, and across a hazy blue sea, the horizon was many kilometres away. He looked towards Zoe Bay, but the beach and the creek mouth at the southern end weren't visible. All he could see were the mangroves and palm forest behind it.

Looking to the north, he saw, three or four kilometres away, the saddle that led to Nina Beach. It didn't look easy going. With several ridges and a forested valley to get through, it wouldn't be the quickest way back to the boat. But it might just keep him alive.

Bad thoughts crowded his head. What if Murderman was hiding near the track and followed him to the boat? Seth swallowed, but his mouth was bone dry. There were two knives and the gaff hook on the boat, but against the reach of the Machet 15, the knives wouldn't be much chop, and the gaff's handle wouldn't survive the first swing at it.

Whatever he did, he couldn't get too close. He'd need to throw rocks or peg a knife right into the bastard's eye. Or smash the bottle of grappa on him, then hurl the lit Zippo . . . which was actually a bloody good idea.

He almost laughed. Well, that's lively, he thought. Now you're planning on burning a man to death. After the bliss of the LSD trip, it felt shocking. But that freak's machine-like attack was also shocking. It put the willies up him. Truth was, he'd light up the bastard if he had to.

Then gunshots flogged the hot air, a string of big booms coming from Zoe Bay. One, two, very fast, then two more the same; a short pause, then one more large-calibre shot.

He leapt to his feet and pointlessly listened for screams and shouts. His heart skipped beats; he heard a moan. He fell back onto the grass, moaned again, then listened to the silence and the gunshots still echoing in his head.

Staying positive, with an eye out for any possibility of changing bad to good, had seen him through a lot of bad times. It had sustained him these last couple of hours. But now a pit had opened beneath him, and he wasn't at all sure that he wasn't going to fall right to the bottom of it.

White Rabbit

That Chinese bastard was right – power came from the barrel of a gun. Bringing a firebomb to a gunfight wasn't going to cut it. And there might be more guns, even a rifle with a scope. He couldn't fight that. This was a complete kick in the guts, a heavy dose of a new reality. Things had gone from bad to much, much worse.

He got up, stood in a daze. Gusts of wind turned his sweat cold. He slapped himself in the face, the shock of it good, then set off, using the open ground to move fast. Twenty minutes later, he saw a little valley opening up ahead of him, and soon he was confronted by a steep gully that he had to cross. The gully's edges were eroded, with crumbling rock, hardy bushes, and small trees all the way down. Peering into the gully, he sensed that the bottom was some distance away.

He went into the gully backwards, hanging off knurled shrubs and branches, his boots sliding on loose stones and dirt. Battling gravity, he took it a few steps at a time, stopping frequently to assess the slope below. All in all, it wasn't so bad; there was lots to hang onto, and there'd be a creek bed down there, maybe a pool of water, even a trickle, and that would be real bloody nice because his thirst now was like a monkey on his back.

Looking down past his legs for the next footholds, his visual focus got thrown. The slope wasn't quite there, but it was. With a lurch of fear, he saw that he'd climbed to the edge of a precipice, its edge hidden by bush and grass.

Climbing back up a few metres, he moved along the top of the cliff face. There was lots of loose rock, and he went higher to avoid it. Squeezing under branches, clambering around impenetrable bushes, he finally got past the drop and resumed his descent.

It grew darker the further down he went, the sunlight not making it into the ravine. He smelt it first, then heard it. Water was dripping from a sheer rock face, the granite covered in green slime and moss. More than grateful, he scrabbled down next to it. Putting his lips to the wet rock, the slime soft against his mouth, he drank like an animal. It took some time, but he filled his belly, and when he began climbing down again, the water sloshed in his gut.

He saw the tops of king ferns below him and knew the bottom wasn't far now. It grew damper, with more rock exposed, and he used small outcrops as handholds. Each time he grabbed a rock, he gave it a shake first to test its strength.

Skidding down another step, he grabbed a rock, found it firm, then let go of the sapling he was hanging from. As the rock took his weight, it came out like a rotten tooth. One boot skidded off its perch. He teetered for a second, then gravity pulled him out backwards into space.

Acutely aware of how fragile his spine was, he twisted it away from the ground, turning like a cat. He jerked his fists and forearms up to shield his head and face and crashed through branches. He bounced off a tree trunk, his upper back taking the force, then he free-fell for crazy seconds before thumping hard into the ground.

He didn't feel it happen, but he must have got knocked out. When he came to, he smelt something awful: a stench like the Devil had shat himself, and right by his shoulder a big head came into focus – monstrous and beady-eyed.

He instinctively jerked away as the head struck at him, the stinking pink gulf of its mouth studded with curved-back teeth. Rolling away, he banged his head into rock, then leapt up. At his groin the monster head flashed in, and he now saw the granddaddy goanna that was at the bottom of the gully with him, the bastard looking to be twenty pounds or more.

Dodging the strike, Seth rolled across the hard edges of the gully, blindly bashing over a boulder's edge, all-out trying to put as much rock between him and the big lizard as possible. Its carnivore mouth slopped with bacteria, and its bite ripped deep: a single nick of its teeth would poison his blood.

The goanna had to know how big he was, but it attacked again, its razor claws rattling across rock. With no time to look for a weapon, Seth leapt into the air, throwing out his arms. He thumped down, then leapt again.

The goanna's head jerked up in surprise. It saw the size of the human now, and it turned and scarpered, its heavy body smashing through fallen branches.

In full pronto mode, Seth ran the other way for a good few metres before he stopped. Leaning against the wall of the gully, he ran his hands over his head. Relief drenched him. He couldn't vouch for what was going on inside it, but his skull was still in one piece.

Keeping alert for the goanna's return, he felt himself for wounds. There was a nice cut on a bicep and other gouges and lumps of varying size. His legs had collected branches on the way down, one leaving a fifty-cent-piece-sized hole in a calf. And he'd taken a real dong to his scone.

Taking a minute, he checked his balance and vision, but he didn't feel concussed. Still, he'd keep tabs on it. Then he shuddered in horror. Lying there unconscious from the fall, he'd been wide-open to attack, the easiest prey. If it wasn't for the bastard's bad breath shocking him awake, he would have suffered a truly horrible death.

Getting his face torn off would have left him blind and choking on blood. How long he'd last then, with blood loss and septic shock, while the big, old lizard waited to mount him for a feed, didn't bear thinking about.

It took a fair bit to get out of the gully, the steep, broken, overgrown ground forcing him to go back on his tracks again and again. He slipped a few times but managed not to fall back down. Knackered, battered, his head aching, he finally came out onto an open, grassy slope.

Still hundreds of metres up, he saw how far he'd come and how bloody far he had to go, and his knees went weak. He flopped down on the soft grass and leaned back on a monolithic granite slab.

The sky told him there wasn't enough light for him to get to Nina Beach now, and the Submariner confirmed it. Damn it to buggery. He'd wasted hours in that gully. It felt like mission over, that he'd done his dash, and he lay there feeling his cuts, scrapes, and bruises throb and tingle. Gratefully occupied by the pain, he let exhaustion, mental and physical, pull him under.

He awoke in a spasm of fear, feeling someone standing over him with a raised blade. But it was pitch black, and a cold wind hissed through the grass and moaned along the rock faces.

He'd been dreaming of a woman, a wrinkled old bird who wasn't too happy, real pissed off in fact. He couldn't remember her face, but her rough voice still rasped in his head, sounding as local as someone from Cardwell or Lucinda.

Curling up against the wind, the grass mercifully soft, he waited to go back under. He kept his thoughts at bay by conjuring up some of the good things he'd felt on the LSD, and it seemed to do the trick.

A faint line of light woke him. He sat up stiff and cold, his legs aching, every cut and scrape stinging, and saw the horizon resolving out of blackness. Across the valley, the colossal shapes of ranges and peaks appeared, traced in gold by the light rolling in from the Coral Sea.

Shaking off sleep took some effort. He stood, stretched, felt the nip in the air. The sun burst free of the horizon, and fire poured from between the clouds manifesting out of the darkness. Rocks appeared, the air vibrating with light, and all round him shadows took on colours.

Everything came into an incredible razor-sharp focus. It was as if he was seeing for the first time. The sky glowed crimson and orange; the green slope shimmered, and the grey ramparts of rocks pulsed with rings and dots of pale lichen. Each blade of grass shivered in gusts of wind, and an intensity filled his senses.

He could smell the ocean from up here and feel the peaks above him humming. His aches and pains receded. It was a new day; who knows, maybe his last, and this possibility blew through him like a divine wind. Breathing slow and deep, he savoured each second – every moment a gift – and he knew the miracle of the holy instant once more.

It didn't last: how could it with what was going on, and he reluctantly looked down at the glittering platinum of Zoe Bay. Through the glare at its southern end, he made out dark specks on the water. It was too bright to see, and he waited as the light changed.

Blinking through the sun's hard glitter, he now saw the masts of two yachts, and that was a surprise. Wouldn't putting as much distance between themselves and the island be a priority? Dread came bubbling back through him. Surely the bastards would think he was long gone. They couldn't still be searching for him?

What he knew for sure was that with no food for close to two days, a raging thirst, and a range of wounds ready to get infected, he had to get to the boat, and soon. With a groan he set off, his boots squeaking on the dewy grass, and his aches and pains came back with a vengeance. Rock faces looked down on him, and he felt like an ant moving through the landscape.

Gauging the terrain ahead, he saw the valley and the saddle above Nina Beach, and he set the saddle's location against the rising sun, as he'd lose sight of it when he went back into the jungle. He'd use gaps in the forest canopy to calculate the sun's position, and that would keep him on track. He couldn't afford to get lost now.

Moving at a jog, he kept above the tree line, avoiding descending into the dark slog of the jungle for as long as he could, and within an hour, the open ground began to fall away as the edge of the valley drew close.

Moving fast, he slipped and almost went headfirst into a rock. Sitting up, he felt unreasonable despair crush him. He'd taken a wee tumble, that's all, but the unfairness, the downright injustice of his situation, was just too much.

He felt dizzy, he felt spent, he felt done. He felt like a fly stuck to the bottom of a wet bucket. It had all turned to absolute shit so bloody fast. And it had been so beautiful. Who in hell would believe this?

It was so crazy – he laughed, and the incredulousness in his voice made him laugh louder. He raised his hands up like an Innisfail cane farmer and said in a thick Italian accent – "Whyyyy? Whyyyy?"

That cracked him up even more, and he laughed until tears ran down his face. The release the laughter gave him was a real shot in the arm, and he got to his feet feeling a damn sight better than he did a minute ago. It probably couldn't get much worse right now, but if it did, well, he'd laugh about it. What the fuck else could he do?

He knew crossing the valley would be hard, but actually doing it was another thing. Trying to travel as the crow flies didn't go as planned. It took him hour after hour, with thirst and hunger sapping his strength. In the dense undergrowth of the valley floor, it was dirty, sweaty work.

As he struggled along, he thought about his father and his mates, that generation of blokes who had gone tired and hungry for weeks and months on end in the jungles of New Guinea while the sons of Nippon tried to kill them, and somehow their plight gave him a bit more strength.

It was a pleasant shock when he emerged onto a ridge and saw the saddle just a few hundred metres away. He picked up the pace, and the back of his shirt was sopping when he came out below the saddle. With aching legs, he slunk through the scrub, eyes scouring the ground ahead, ears alert for any sound.

Through tussocks of wallaby grass he caught a glimpse of a gap between the stems – the track – and he crept up to it and stopped. Lying in the grass, he listened, sniffing the air like an animal. After a few minutes he got up and went along the track to the crest of the saddle. From there he looked at Zoe Bay and saw the white sliver of beach at the southern end. But the yachts were gone, and for a second he wondered if he'd even seen them at all.

His stomach made a piteous sound, and he jogged down off the saddle and hurried through the trees. When he saw the blue of the sea, he slowed right down. Coming into the back of Nina Beach, he got off the track and crept through stands of pandanus and casuarina. Edging closer, his eyes homed in on the spot amongst the beach almonds where he'd left the Starcraft, and, man, what a sight for sore eyes – it was still there.

He watched the red boulders at the end of the beach. Someone there with a scoped rifle could easily shoot him. Or would Murderman rush him as he came up to the boat? Like with most things, there was only one way to find out.

As he went through the trees to the Starcraft, no one rushed at him with a bush knife, but the anticipation of being turned into molecules of light by a hundred and fifty grains of lead sent a stupendous rush through him.

At the boat, he stood by the gunwale and knew that at this moment he was both dead and alive. The salt-tang smell of the sea was strong. Pandanus leaves rattled in a stiff breeze. Live in the here and now, he thought, and you live forever.

Seconds passed. His stomach grumbled. He undid the tarp, got a cup, and filled it from the water drum. He drank it down and did it again. Then he fell on the food.

In a mad trance, he wolfed down dates, peanut butter, bread, cabin crackers, and cheese. He ate a tomato in two bites, juice running from his mouth, then crunched up a bar of chocolate. It was like the best drugs he'd ever had.

Finally sated, he stopped and sat there, stunned by the food. He didn't have words to describe it, but he could feel the nourishment moving through him, firing up synapses and turning switches back on.

He got the spark plug, put it back in, then opened the fuel line. He checked the Submariner, saw it was almost ten. He looked at the sea. Whitecaps crested, tall clouds rode along. He grabbed sponge and soap, ran naked into the sea, and every cut and gouge screamed blue murder. Moaning with pain, he carefully cleaned himself.

Back at the boat, throbbing like a bastard, he swallowed six Disprin, then dressed his cuts with mercurochrome and some of his aunt's salve. Sealing the biggest cuts and holes with plasters, he put on clean clothes, and the smell of laundered cotton was like civilisation itself.

Now he'd evolved from a filthy, desperate ape-man to semi-human; he was ready to go. It had taken him a day and a night to get here, but what was he going to do now?

He should stay out of it, go to the resort, and get them to radio the Cardwell cops. But he knew he couldn't do that. Not yet. What he'd seen at Zoe Bay now compelled him to go back. He had to know.

But doing that and getting out again in one piece came down to three things: Were they still there, did he have the fastest boat, and did they have a rifle? Finding all that out could get him taken off the board.

Weighing it up, he stared at the water – and saw a speck of colour appear in the south. Resisting the urge to stand and look, he froze and saw the orange-hulled yacht come into view.

A kilometre or more out, it had its sails up, catching the brisk sou-easterly. Making good time, he reckoned they were using their engine as well. He sat like a sniper in a hide, watching the yacht cruise past, and sure enough, he heard the faint throb of a marine engine.

The yacht looked bigger than *Vicarious*. There could be three, even four, of the bastards onboard. The decks were empty, but there was someone in the cockpit, but without his binoculars he couldn't see much more.

It took the yacht a few minutes to disappear behind the next headland. He waited for *Vicarious* to appear, but it didn't. He drank more water, then shook his head.

Who in God's name were these people? They had just turned up, relentless killers who did whatever the bloody hell they wanted, sure in the knowledge that no one would ever find out what they'd done.

Remembering a quote from a pirate comic, he mouthed it: '*Because piracy is done in remote and solitary places, where the weak and defenseless can expect no assistance or relief, these devils in their wantonness of power add cruelty to theft.*'

He knew there were modern-day pirates in Southeast Asia. He'd heard it on the news and from a mate of Pep's who'd sailed in the Philippines and Indonesia. But those bastards operated up there, not in far north Queensland.

Then he flashed on Murderman: his otherworldliness. The muscled-up freak hadn't said boo. He'd been like a wind-up toy. Just a bloke in shorts, with a crewcut and a sailor tattoo. But somehow he hadn't felt Australian.

Yeah. He was another Yank. And he wasn't a pirate, not like that. He'd come here *because* of Jack and Elinore.

He flashed on Jack whispering in the dark, '*He's here,*' sounding like he was about to kak his daks. And Elinore. For all her spunk and confidence, she'd been scared too, of something vague and unspecified that he'd been too out of his head to understand.

Torn deep with regret, he shouted in wordless grief. You should have told me! Trusted me! I could have hidden you in a dozen places! Double damnation and fuck it to hell!

Jumping to his feet, he knocked the anguish away and concentrated hard. The orange yacht was going north, to Cairns or some other anchorage, or maybe to the Grafton Passage and back out into the Coral Sea. He'd go into Zoe Bay now, and if it came back, he'd outrun it. Otherwise, he'd see what he had to see, then tail the yacht north.

He dragged the Starcraft into the water. The engine fired up first go and he headed out of the bay. Out on the horizon, a mass of cumulus clouds was stacking up, the edge of some weather out on the reef.

He cleared the point and turned south. Heading into the wind, the Starcraft bounced across the water. He drove hard along the headland that formed the northern side of Zoe Bay. Along its high cliffs, fingers of granite stuck out, forming rugged little coves.

He gave the Evinrude more gas, eyes straining for the southern end of Zoe Bay to appear. When it did, he looked towards the creek mouth – but *Vicarious* wasn't there. Dark things skittered around his head. No, no, no, mate, he told himself. You don't know anything yet.

Coming into the bay, it looked even more remote, even more mythical than when he'd seen it all those years ago. But he could see the big valley where he'd nearly become goanna food and the palm forest that Murderman had chased him through. And he heard the brutal finality of those gunshots again. It was a different place now.

Turning parallel with the beach, he sped towards the creek, the paranoia of what he'd find there burrowing into him like a tick. Aiming for where the track came out a few hundred metres from the creek, he scanned the tree line there for reflections or for someone coming out onto the sand. But nobody did nothing, and he brought the boat in to the beach, killed the engine, and the boat hissed onto the sand.

Hopping out, he fought trepidation. Showing his teeth and growling like a dog helped, and as he walked towards the creek, his eyes combed the beach ahead. Breathing deeply through his nose, he listened for flies and gave any log or big enough pile of flotsam a second look.

At the tree where he'd hung it, his rucksack lay slashed up on the sand. Murderman had gone to town on it. His binoculars were rent with blows, the lenses starred, and the dope tin, though intact, was badly dented. What a big baby, thought Seth.

In the grove of trees where they'd camped, he moved slowly, looking around at the sand. He saw footprints, but nothing else. He went through the trees and looked at the beach by the creek. The sand there looked disturbed. Flies worked an area. He went to it and sifted sand with his fingers – and saw dry clots of brown. He stood and quickly brushed his hands off. From a thousand fishing trips, he knew it was blood.

Using his feet, he moved sand about, and – bingo – saw a flash of brass. He crouched and picked up a pistol shell. Stamped into its base was the legend .45 Colt. From the gun club he knew these rounds went off with a real bang.

He looked out at the calm, green water of the creek. A faint breeze ruffled its surface. Closer to the shore he saw a black mulch of leaves and branches on the bottom of the creek. And there was something pale in there. His scalp prickled. It looked like skin.

He went to the edge and stared through the crystal-clear water. In the decayed mat of vegetation he could see the curves of a calf muscle and the back of a knee, the pale flesh luminous in the sunlight. Jesus.

Then a metre away – more glimpses of skin amongst the dark mulch. His synapses jumped. Shivers zapped him. He wanted it to be a hallucination, but it wasn't. He was looking at a second body.

A breeze rustled the trees behind him. Up the creek a bird called. Bad vibrations crawled all over him at the thought of what he was going to have to do now. It would be a real horrorshow – but he had to know.

He got his rucksack, ran back to the boat, and chucked it in. He grabbed his mask and snorkel and sprinted back to the creek. He washed the mask out, fitted it, then slid into the warm water. Swimming across the sand, he took a big breath, submerged, and slowly swam over the thick snarl of leaves to where he'd seen the bodies.

Skin peeked from between leaves. Reflections from the sun threw shifting patterns of light over suntanned flesh that looked soft and vulnerable, a curve like a hip. He saw a bit of green material. He tried to remember if he'd seen Elinore wearing anything that colour.

Now he saw a big red hole in the flesh – a bullet wound. He couldn't believe it, didn't want to believe it, but like all the bad shit that kept happening, it was all too real.

A leaf by the body moved, and a mangrove jack swam out, a scrap of pink fluttering in its mouth. Seth now saw more shreds of pink suspended in the water. His stomach jumped. Pushing back against the shouting in his head, he focused on looking in the mat of debris for a stick so he could clear the leaves away and see.

Nearby the light suddenly changed. Something moving underwater. He turned, saw a big, dark shape swimming towards him: a wide body and clawed legs, and a jagged, undulating tail propelling it forward at speed.

Swerving sideways, Seth swam hard at the white slump of the creek bank, bolts of electricity spiking through his arms and legs. He hit the sand underwater, feet sinking in, grabbing purchase, and he leapt upwards, bursting through the water into the sunlight.

Then he was on hot white sand, scrambling up to the trees. Hearing only the thud of his feet, he stopped and ripped the mask off. Looking back, he saw no big bastard crocodile chasing him, just the ripples of his escape.

Watching the creek, he let a sense of what-the-fuck-just-happened catch up with him. Water dripped off him onto the sand. He buzzed, ready to run again, but the croc wasn't going to come out of the creek for him; it was too busy guarding its windfall.

As the adrenaline subsided, an abject sadness tore him up, the senselessness of what had happened wailing in his head. It was just so brutal, abrupt, and final. No burial, no funeral: just fish and crocodiles eating their fill.

He battled the grief hard, smashed it down and kicked it away. Yeah, okay. He'd got the news; he knew the score. It was time to stop acting like a big girl and sort out a plan. But he didn't feel too sharp. He'd been acid-washed and wrung out, and his brain felt like a punching bag.

He went to the boat, got the rum, and took a few belts. He tried for thoughts and meanings, but nothing came. It was like the vacancy he'd felt on the LSD, but behind it now lurked an intense darkness, not calmness and light. He felt the void pulling at him, and he made himself look around and consciously take in his surroundings.

On the horizon an armada of clouds was piling up in the southeast, the sky growing dark there. In the bay the sea shimmered endlessly in the sun. On the headland beyond the creek, waves crashed into rocks, sending up sheets of spray. Concentrating hard, he noted details.

Row after row of waves came in, some with whitecaps, and there – a quick glimpse of red in the water. He stood up and watched the spot. Then, almost beyond his field of vision, he saw it again.

He quickly got going, standing in the Starcraft to keep his eyes on the flash of red appearing and disappearing in the water, and it was a good few minutes before he could see what was floating out there – a red jerrycan.

Up close, he dropped his speed right down and netted it. Barely full, the jerrycan looked fairly new. There were some numbers and letters stamped into the bottom of it, but nothing to say where it came from.

With the Starcraft starting to turn side-on to the waves, he quickly unscrewed the lid and smelt fuel. He hadn't seen the jerrycan on *Vicarious'* deck or in the inflatable; it must have been below deck. Screwing the lid back on, he put it with his gear and kept heading out of the bay. Five minutes later, he saw something else.

A tiny flash of white, much smaller than the jerrycan, and he had to really focus hard to keep it in sight. It wasn't easy, even using the rocky shore as a reference point, and he lost it numerous times before he got close. Dropping the speed to near zero, he went in, the prop growling in the chop. It took a few tries, but he got it into the boat.

There in the mesh of the net was the little white plastic rabbit he'd seen above the companionway on *Vicarious*.

Waves smacked into the side of the boat; his head and chest felt hollow. Another wave pounded in; he nearly fell. Grabbing the throttle, he fired up the engine and drove on out to the end of the headland.

At the point was a big hillock of steep cliffs, joined to the headland by a low strip of sand and scrub. The sea was moving, the swell rolling in, and clouds completely filled the southeastern sky. In the distance on the mainland, he could see the white specks of the sheds and sugar wharf at Lucinda bright below the big grey sky.

Turning in the surging sea, he cruised around in an ever-widening circle, the boat jumping and bucking as his eyes sifted through shifting blue and green.

Then he saw a sheen in the water – a small slick of oil. When he got to it, he wallowed in the swell at slow speed. He was a few kilometres off the point now. He knew from the map that it dropped right off here many fathoms deep. He stared at the dirty rainbow. He knew what it meant. *Vicarious* was out here. The bastards had sealed her up before they sunk her, but a few things had got away.

Stunned by the finality of it, he circled aimlessly. He felt detached, the immensity of the sea and sky a million miles away. When a wave smashed over the side, spraying him with cold water, he was grateful for its shock.

The roar of the Evinrude filled his head as he drove the ten minutes back. On the beach waves foamed across the sand, and the wind clamoured in the trees. His cuts and gashes stung as he pulled the Starcraft up the beach a few metres. The tide was coming in, but he wouldn't be long.

He looked at the creek and the grove of trees. It wasn't right just leaving them there like this, but without a rifle, he was buggered. A dinosaur ruled the creek. The cold fact of the impermanence of the corporeal world sent a steel-hard punch through him. Death had been here, and there was nothing he could do. Except go get Pep's folding shovel.

With his boots back on and shovel in hand, he hurried onto the track. A few hundred meters in, he began looking for the ridge he'd explored for caves. When he saw its dark bulk in the trees, he left the track and raced towards it.

Slipping through the repetitive shapes and tones of the forest, he ransacked his memory. The ridge loomed, and leaves and twigs crackled as he moved along next to the rising ground. He saw an indentation in the terrain: a dry creek bed coming down the ridge, and he ran it. He looked at the jumble of rocks vanishing into the forest, then at the trees, then at the ridge again.

Something clicked, and he went back towards the beach and soon saw the long dead branch festooned with purple coral pea and the stand of she-oaks he'd used as cover. A mental picture began resolving in his mind's eye, and he scrambled forward, then slowed right down.

He eyeballed the vegetation, saw the broken end of the banksia branch, its dead leaves. He went and stood with his back to it and found the other branch he'd snapped in two. He looked down and saw the disturbed soil under the leaf litter. Unfolding the shovel, he began to dig.

Within seconds the shovel hit something. Scraping the dark earth away, Seth uncovered the tops of two black plastic cases. They looked like big power tool cases, and he flashed that there were handguns inside them.

There was a rumble from the ocean, and an insect buzz started up. On his knees, he tried to use the shovel to lever a case up, but it was too heavy. He cleared the dirt around it, revealing a handle. He put his hand through the grip and lifted, and the weight shocked him. The case must weigh twenty kilos.

It took both hands to get it out. Dumping it flat on the ground, he saw there was no lock, just two heavy-duty sliding clips. He opened the case and saw why it was so heavy. It was full of gold bars.

In the second case there were more gold bars and a large Ziploc satchel. Inside the satchel were four smaller plastic Ziploc bags, each one containing a big, flat book. He took one out and leafed through it. Even in the half-light of the forest, the full-colour plates were compelling, the pictures filled with imagery he'd never imagined, let alone seen. They were right out of an LSD trip.

Between the pages were sheets of thick white paper, obviously protection for the colour plates. He flipped through the pages, running his fingers down to the seams, checking for money, documents, photographs, or letters. He didn't find anything, but to be completely sure, he quickly went through the other books the same way.

Well, now you know, he thought. That's why they were murdered in cold blood. And why a complete stranger had tried to cut his head off. Gold.

He'd seen it up on the Cape, even in Cairns: how a good amount of the stuff could send blokes crazy. It really was heavy stuff. But those bastards hadn't found it. A terrible image of torture and doomed defiance flashed through his mind, and he smashed it away.

Sweat trickled down his neck. From the sea came another rumble. Something cracked nearby. He looked around. Seconds later came another crack. Then on the next sharp snap, he saw a seedpod on an acacia tree release tiny seeds that fell to the ground.

With a sudden buzz, an insect flew into his eye, slid into the corner of it, and began burrowing under his eyelid. He shattered its body picking it out, and the sting and acrid smell told him it was a stink bug.

Tears spurted as he tried to get all the fragments out. With thumb and forefinger he plucked and wiped, finally removing most of it. He rubbed his eye, and it stung like hell. He'd have to flush it properly with water when he got back to the boat.

Blinking away tears, he hefted the cases in both hands. The handles looked like they'd never been intended to lug real weight. The edges were sharp, cutting into his hands, and he had to take several breaks to rest them, each time rubbing his damn eye.

Heaven & Hell

On the beach wind gusts batted his face and ears. The mouth of the bay had darkened, and above the sea was a tall mass of dark clouds, the highest tops lit white by the sun. Behind them the sky was a deep grey.

Seth got the cases to the boat, then grabbed the canteen and flushed his eye. It was itchy beyond belief, the nerve endings tingling like buggery.

Lightning forked pink over the iron blue sea. Thunder boomed. He lifted the cases on board. He felt dizzy. The last two days had really tested him. Moving fast, he undid the tarp, stowed the cases on either side of the hull for balance, then tied it all down nice and tight.

Looking back at the sweep of beach, he suddenly saw Elinore and Jack standing right there, smiling sweetly at him. He felt a great rush of emotion at this hallucination of the heart, and he knew this vision would haunt him for the rest of his life.

He pulled the Starcraft into the sea and, with a shock, saw, like he had x-ray eyes, dozens of creatures – rays, eels, fish – all swimming in the opaque water around him.

Shaking this weirdness off, he hopped in behind the wheel. The sky buzzed, the sea hummed, visible electricity rippled through the air. He was feeling very strange now, and he knew it must be a result of all that had happened to him here physically, mentally, and emotionally.

Waves slapped the boat. Thunder drummed against the mountains, the sound reverberating up and down valleys. It sounded like the island was talking, like it was angry. He fired up the engine. He gave it gas. With an extra forty kilos onboard, the boat began punching through waves.

The sky ahead didn't look so good now. Dark as the arse end of Satan, it boiled black and green, and evil tendrils of cloud were reaching down.

Going hard across the bay, he looked back at the island, at the wall of rock stark against the blue sky, at the strip of white beach below, and where The Thumb erupted out of the range, he saw a huge face, alive and aware, its eyes deep in rock, its mouth a black shadow cut into the sheer escarpment. The mouth moved, the eyes widened, and the mountain looked right at him.

Jesus in a cane train, he thought. I'm hallucinating like crazy, and it's as strong as before! The LSD had come back with a vengeance. Maybe this San Francisco acid double-dipped your brain. Heart racing, he turned back to the storm, and something went off, exploding in his head, and he saw perfectly sized diamonds in every moving wave and felt the wind pluck at him with busy fingers.

Black clouds overran the sky. The bay became a million shades of grey, the water a maelstrom of steely shards. It looked like a drawing from a cataclysmic myth. From his buzzing toes to the top of his expanding head, Seth felt the untamed power of the sea flexing around him, lifting and buffeting the boat. The headlands looked closer, but they faded to grey as the first squall line came in. Then a huge rush of acid hit him, everything dissolving into light for an endless second, and he hung on like fuck to the wheel.

From all around came a gigantic boom, F-111-sized, and a lightning bolt hit the sea right off the hillock point: a cone of light that lit up the surging sea around it. Reeling in shock, he knew it was a sign, and he slowed to a stop.

The sky was the blackest eye, a whole ocean of rain up there. A howling wind hit, waves smashing into the hull. He felt like he was in one of those plastic snowflake globes, about to be shaken.

Frustration burned through him. He'd run out of time. He couldn't get off the island now. Rapidly spiralling into an LSD whirlpool, he'd go down in this storm. It was the biggest bit of bullshit thrown at him yet, but he turned the boat around and pulled back on the throttle.

Flying back to the beach, he hit top speed, the Evinrude a banshee scream. On the cliffs and peaks ahead of him, crazy faces and bodies pulsated and writhed. Around the Starcraft things leapt into the air, sea creatures of shapes and colours he'd never seen before, their luminous bodies crackling with electricity.

At the periphery of his vision he saw a big flash, then thunder smote the air. On the north headland, a burning tree fell into the forest. Another chemical rush staggered him. Trying to keep his mental pants on, he scrambled for a rational thought, and he made the boat the most important thing, and he said it again and again in his head – *the boat, the boat, the boat.*

Every wave had a whitecap now. Raindrops hit his back. He turned, saw a huge curtain of rain rushing into the bay, clouds falling out of the sky. The sea around the boat suddenly exploded with falling water that smashed down onto his head and shoulders. Visibility vanished; white spray and grey mist engulfed him, and the world shrunk to the bench seat, the wheel, and the throttle. And it was fine by him.

Things were real simple now, everything reduced to the things that absolutely counted. He was rushing through water, wind, space, and time. It was stark, elemental. Only the now mattered, and he could just about handle that.

Fighting to maintain his sanity – *the boat, the boat, the boat* – he came in on the squall line; the rain almost solid, the beach rushing up, and with a huge mental effort, he cut the engine. Impossibly, the roar of the rain and wind was louder than the din the outboard had been making.

Speeding forward, the boat held steady. Grabbing for logic, he scrambled to the engine, released the tiller pin, wrenched the motor up, and locked it off. Seconds later the Starcraft hit the beach.

Rationality was collapsing. His vision was turning in on itself. Subatomic structures and organic networks flooded his head. Wham! A wave slammed into the boat, spinning it about, tipping it to one side. He fell, lolling against the gunwale.

As everything melded into meaninglessness, the storm surge hammered into the boat, and he leapt to the wave-lashed beach, ears booming in the rush of wind and rain. His feet sank into sand, and whump! – the boat slammed into him, knocking him into the foaming water. Waves thudded in, throwing the prow up over him. As the boat slammed down, he rolled sideways through the surf and scrambled to his feet.

The deluge was horizontal; he couldn't see. The wind began to flog the palm forest and foothills. Over the rising tumult came wild gunshots: the cracks of branches being blown off trees. Lightning lit the clouds rushing overhead.

With his head an erupting Roman candle, Seth grabbed the anchor rope, and on autopilot now, a flesh-and-bone machine, he dragged the Starcraft up the short stretch of beach. Staggering forward, he heard the wind ramp up, its tone changing, and over the roar came a deep, sonorous sound as the storm slammed into the mountain range.

Coherent thought flatlined. He let go of whatever it was in his hands and fell to the sand. With a final spasm of energy, he crawled into the flimsy cover of the tree line. Rolling onto his back, he lay still, and with his eyes shut against the stinging rain, let oblivion storm his mind.

A million raindrops made a single hard tone: a belting sizzle. Acid blew through him in coruscating splendour, a non-stop, white-hot eruption exploding and re-exploding in incandescent fury. He felt his mind blow away, his body dissolve as he disintegrated into atoms of water and light.

Completely integrated into the moment, he spun in an endless loop. Infinity claimed him, but this time it felt incredibly dense, dark, and compressed, spiralling in on itself like a horrid, black, indestructible thread.

He tried to move – his arms, his legs, his fingers – but he was caught in cold, ancient rock. Paranoia choked him; primal fear crushed down. He was completely helpless, at the mercy of anything that came along. The crocodile in the creek, Murderman and his mates, any nasty bastard from anywhere – they could all take him now. Paralysed, screaming silently, he felt them coming.

Like fingers, the rain tapped his legs. A falling branch slapped his chest. Faces appeared out of the rain. A boot hammered into his neck. Another broke his nose. They jostled around to get at him, stamping down hard. He felt his bones break, his flesh tear. They murdered him with machetes, chains, hammers, knives, and guns. A laughing bastard tightly held his head, while his mate pounded a cold chisel deep into his mouth.

His fear and pain grew as he saw how endless it was. All over the world: fathers beaten to death in front of their families, mothers raped and killed, daughters sold into slavery, sons castrated, hospitals bombed, cities shelled, and children and babies burnt alive.

And right here on this beach: Elinore raped, bashed, and humiliated, her spirit crushed by cruel men. He saw Jack bludgeoned, maimed, and tortured. He saw and felt the evil games played before they were murdered. He knew their terror and despair.

Fear eviscerated him, and he screamed in awful unison with millions of others. This was the horror of millennia: the primordial heart of man pumping with dark blood, a howling wilderness of search and destroy, pillage, hunt, and kill.

Like crazy old paintings come to life, he saw hundreds of demons, evil-eyed, red-faced, wild, and hairy. Rolling eyes and breathing fire, they brandished weapons as they glared down at him, their rage unforgiving, eternal.

They fell upon him, and he felt cleavers and sticking-pig spears enter his flesh; metal sliding through him, hacking muscle and cracking bone, and with ungodly chanting and roars of contemptuous laughter, the demons roughly hacked him up and threw the pieces to waiting dogs and vultures.

He writhed, clutching for something to fight back with. He saw dozens of pistols, clear as day in the darkness. All he had to do was reach up and grab one. Like pages in a catalogue, rifles and machine guns now appeared, barrels bristling, magazines fat, and he moaned with relief. These things could kill anything out there.

The pages flipped faster, weapon after weapon, and the guns' calibres grew larger and larger, mutating into huge bores that didn't exist. He saw guns that could never be made: triple, quintuple barrels, curved barrels, bent ones, their shapes more and more ludicrous, losing all meaning.

A drumroll of thunder reverberated. Now worms and cockroaches passed through the ground beneath him. The rain streaming off his body felt like a swarm of flies. His eyes stung as bugs and crawlies flew into them and ran their feelers around his eyeballs and under the skin of his cheeks. Centipedes stung hard, pincers sinking into the soft flesh of his neck and groin. Millipedes writhed in his ears and nostrils and crawled into his mouth. Grubs and maggots burrowed and squirmed in his guts.

He was dead. All of him that had been wet and mucous was now dried out. He was a pile of bones in a cocoon of chewed-up clothing, his hair plucked out by birds for their nests, scorpions and slaters living in his dusty skull.

There was something peaceful, almost restful, in this. Beyond him was the world as it always was and would always be. It didn't need him, and in this ending he knew eternity was real. This quietude should have brought some consolation, but the dread of being attacked came back. Terror at his helplessness battered him, and he tried to float again, to meld without thought into the rain.

Then someone was there. Standing over him. His heart leapt. A familiar face was smiling through the pouring rain, and he laughed in joy as he saw the square jaw and mask of the Phantom. He couldn't believe it, but the Ghost Who Walks was right here with him.

But he felt stupid lying there. It was weak, shameful, but the Phantom didn't care. He was cool about it. Then he went to take his mask off, and Seth told him he wasn't allowed to do that. But he did, and Seth almost shat himself. The bastard's eyes looked just like his mask! — flat white diamonds with no eyeballs, watching him like an alien from another planet.

Seth quickly shut his eyes, and a sickening kaleidoscope of Phantoms swirled through his head, every white smile a plunging knife. He tried to float again, failed, felt his body on the sand; gravity implacable. The rain hammered down, an unholy choir of voices all singing one unending note. Now a bass tone filled the air. Something had joined the roar of wind, rain, and thunder.

The tone changed and modulated. He heard a subsonic voice growling — a woman's voice, primal and pitiless. It was terrifying; it was demonic. He didn't understand the words, but he understood their meaning, and an icy spear of anguish went through him.

She'd made the storm, all elements at her command. She could torment him forever or kill him mercifully. But he'd have to submit to her completely before she'd let him die. And he couldn't hold anything back. It would be all or nothing with her.

The overwhelming voice shook him to his bones, and he heard evil laughter in the rolling thunder. The sense of her presence grew, filling the space above his face and chest. She was right there, floating above him, her breasts and belly almost touching him, her mouth close, her breath as cold as ice. Buzzing with terror, he trembled and shook.

At the edge of the void now, about to tumble in, he suddenly found a razor-edged certainty. He didn't have to worry anymore. He didn't have to fight. Someone bigger than everything that was happening was in control, and knowing that she could destroy him, and now wanting it, he let her press her cold lips to his.

Passing As Men

At dawn, with light trying to break through the drizzle, Seth staggered out of the dripping trees onto the beach. The tide was in; the sky a slightly different shade of steel to the ocean. The headlands steamed with mist, and the long beach faded into grey a few hundred metres away.

He looked through the soft rain at the creek mouth and saw a mad rush of brown water punching out into the bay. With the tide right in, standing waves were jumping and bucking at the creek mouth, branches and logs surfing over them.

Standing in the dull light, listening to the roar of the creek, he felt bereft of thought or emotion. He still had one foot deep in the LSD, but he was also here. It felt like the drug might be wearing off, but for how long? This stuff kept coming back like malaria.

At the Starcraft, he stared at the shin-deep water in the bottom of the boat for the longest time. It took a lot more staring before he visualised the drain plug at the bottom of the transom. He staggered around, crouched down by the outboard engine, and undid the plug.

Water spurted out, making a smooth hole in the sand, and he watched vacantly until no more came. After a bit, he screwed the plug back in, then got in the boat.

It took a while, stop-starting and staring into space, to

tie the tarp over the windscreen and onto the cleats on the second divider. Under it, he slowly took off his boots and clothes, then got a towel. After drying himself, he put on long pants, a long-sleeved shirt, and dry socks.

With his feet up on the bench seat and the rain sluicing off the tarp, he sat there enjoying the feeling of being dry and warm. It wouldn't last, but it was fine for now.

After sitting in a dream of absolutely nothing, he had an idea, and it pleased him no end, as it was proof he hadn't lost his marbles. It still took him an age, peering into the gloom under the tarp to find what he needed. Eventually he got the billy going, the gas flame flaring blue on the bench seat next to him.

Floating in space, he put two big tablespoons of cocoa into a mug, then some golden syrup and a big glug of rum. He added boiling water, stirred it well, then drank it like the medicine it was. It saved his life. Then he did it all over again.

It took him another hour to get the Starcraft repacked and seaborne again, his Drizabone raincoat keeping him relatively dry, and this time when he drove out of Zoe Bay, he didn't look back.

Past the headland, he instinctively turned south, the hillock point watching him as he slid by. The sea wasn't easy, but he dug into it, and the engine roar became a part of him. He felt like a machine, and that was good.

He passed a long, long beach, the steaming jungle above it disappearing into cloud. Silver waterfalls appeared in the mist at times, and along the shoreline dead trees lay like big black bodies on the sand. The channel between the island and the mainland came into view, and leaving the waves and wind behind, he drove up it into a world of endless mangroves and drifting mist.

Beyond wired, he floated in a fog of gritty numbness, his body separate from himself, his mind too. Green, grey, green, grey; mangrove, water, and low cloud rolled past, with the occasional creek yawning darkly in the swamp. Something like a year went by.

There were some dinghies, but no boats moored at the jetty at Cardwell. There was no one around either, and it vaguely registered with him as a good thing. But when he came up to the boat ramp, he saw that there was someone there after all: an older bloke of indeterminate race sitting in an aluminium dinghy. Cutting the engine, Seth nosed in and tied off.

"Morning," said the bloke cheerfully. "Bit of a blow last night, aye?"

Seth nodded, unsure if he could speak.

"Yeah, old Kitty," said the bloke, waving at the island.

Seth stared at him. The man grinned.

"She lives up there in the mountains there. Makes the storms. She got the power of the wind and the lightning. Sink you like a stone if she wants. Women, hey?"

He laughed with the wisdom of experience.

Speechless, Seth kept on staring. It didn't make any real sense, but after everything he'd been through, it sounded about right.

Heading back up the Bruce Highway, he was pleased to have the task of driving to occupy his mind. Like the boat trip, it had its own very simple rules, and the repetition of sound and movement kept him on a nice, straight rail.

All the way to Tully, the creeks were up, and the ditches along the highway pulsed with the runoff from last night's storm. Outside of El Arish, a mako blue Monaro overtook him, the muscle car doing a ton, and on the sidewalk at the Mourilyan pub, he saw two bustards having a blue, their big wings spread and long necks darting.

Passing the turnoff to South Johnstone, he thought of the bungalow there, but he had no fish for his mate's freezer. And he also had something that he couldn't just leave lying around.

He got a bit of a shock coming into Cairns. Though he'd never have described it as much more than a sweaty little port at the end of the line, it suddenly felt busy, with cars and trucks buzzing about like big metal insects.

Waiting at the dinging horizontal boom of the railway intersection at the Fiveways, he felt the dread come back. For the first time in hours he had nothing to actually do, and bad things began to darken his mind. He was shocked to see how little he had left to fight back with.

Then, thank Christ, the dinging stopped and someone began leaning on their horn. Jolted out of his daze, he drove across the tracks, took a hard left onto Water Street, and very consciously drove north.

Fifteen kilometres out of town, he turned off the Cook Highway and was soon in the little beachside hamlet of Half Moon Bay. He turned into the caravan park by the beach and drove down to Johnny Pep's spot near the sand. There were boats and dinghies outside caravans, some cars, a panel van, and out the front of Pep's, a green, two-door Torana Six. As he pulled up, he saw the car's owner standing in the caravan door.

He killed the engine, tried out a smile. Pep's girlfriend, Suzy, in shorts and tight t-shirt, smiled in puzzlement. He had to be careful here. Suzy was sharp.

"Well, that was bloody quick," she said. "I thought you might keep it the whole time he was away."

"Um, yeah. I've . . . uh, come back."

His words stumbled along his tongue, his ability to form thoughts shaky. He sounded vulnerable. Suzy took in the nicks and scratches on his face and arms, and he was glad he had a long-sleeved shirt and trousers on.

"Yeah . . . a bit of a storm," said Seth. "Took a tumble. So, if . . . if it's cool, I'll give the boat a clean . . . and take, uh, take a nap."

With bottomless eyes, Suzy contemplated him.

"Yeah, go for it," she said. "I'm off to work later."

He parked under some palm trees, and in their rustling shadows checked out the boat. There were a few dings and scratches, but no proper dents. His head fizzed, his limbs felt heavy, but he was real happy to be doing something. He gave the boat a good hosing, washing it clean, then checked the motor, fuel line, and steering cables.

As he worked, he saw Suzy go to the shower block with a towel and toiletry bag. When she brought over a cuppa, she was dressed in a sleeveless top and a denim skirt, her face made up with mascara, eyeshadow, and lipstick.

"Hooray, it's a Friday night," she said. "Eight hours of watching the grog I dish up turn them into bloody jelly. But they wouldn't have it any other way."

Seth sipped tea. His bones hummed with fatigue.

"You okay, Seth?" said Suzy, and the empathy in her voice brought him close to collapse.

"Bit knackered," he confessed. "The storm . . . and I got on the grog last night . . . and, uh, I saw the dawn."

"More than grog, I'd say," said Suzy. "Listen, the shower key is on the counter in the van, and there's a bit of smoke behind the fridge. Okay? I'll see ya later."

She watched him haul up a smile, but he could tell she didn't buy it. With a tight nod, she got into the Torana. As she pulled out onto the gravel, a freshly lit cigarette in her mouth, her eyes bored into him.

He got the shower block key, and in the cubicle leaned against the concrete wall numbly relishing the hot water. A little rejuvenated, he dressed in his last clean shorts and tended to his wounds, putting mercurochrome and a fresh plaster on the hole in his calf. Then he got his swag out of the Starcraft and laid it out on the shady grass next to the boat.

He lay down on it and wallowed in a blessed feeling of cleanliness. In the afternoon sun, with the sound of the sea and shorebirds, he felt a profound pleasure at being able to stop now. And best of all, his mind felt empty. With a deep sigh, he closed his eyes and crashed right out.

He awoke in shock. It was night, and a face was close to his, half lit by the caravan annex a few metres away. A swathe of darkness was sliding up his body, brushing along his legs and chest.

He sat up fast, nearly knocking heads with Suzy. Behind her the light by the mango tree jumped with insects. He smelt wood smoke, and from a van site somewhere close came the soft laughter of mates sharing a joke.

All legs, Suzy was squatting by him. In shorts and a t-shirt again, she was pulling a cover over him. He'd always fancied her, and he knew she'd thought about it too, but they both loved Pep too much to try anything. But right now he wanted to snuggle right into her.

"Hey, sleepyhead," she said. He tried to fully wake up, not happy at feeling this groggy.

"Jesus, Seth," she said. "You got some good knocks and holes in you. You get in a fight out there?"

Unwilling to speak, he shrugged. Unsatisfied with this, she opened her mouth, but then she sighed and gently pushed him back down into his swag. You're an angel, he thought, looking past her smooth arms at her lovely face.

She slowly shook her head like he was a wayward child.

"You sleep now," she said. "You need it."

Smoothing the cover against his shoulder, she left her hand there. Seth, fully compos now, wanted to pour out the last two days to her, but the nonstop awfulness of it had mucked him up. He didn't have the words to describe it now. He felt an incoherence that only time would clear.

And even if he could tell her, he wouldn't. Involving her in this bad trip of violence and death was not on. Maybe he'd tell Pep about it down the track, way down the track, but not her.

She stood up and looked down at him.

"You look like you've seen something," she said.

Yeah, he thought. The fucking elephant.

Waking up outdoors was something he'd done since he was a kid. But here at Half Moon Bay, with a gentle sea breeze and sunlight flickering through the palm fronds, it felt especially nice.

Seth sat up and looked around. There was a woman in

shorts and a floral blouse pegging up laundry, and up the road a bit, a fella was working on an HG Holden. It all looked reassuringly normal, and he needed a bit of that.

From the position of the sun, he saw he'd been out for a good while, and the Submariner confirmed it – nearly ten hours. The Torana had gone, Suzy up and about, and he lay back and cautiously examined his mind.

The big sleep had done him a power of good. It felt like the jiggery-pokery of the LSD had faded. And best of all, the debilitating fear had gone. That had been a killer.

Lying there paralysed in the storm at Zoe Bay with his brains running out onto the sand, he had really thought he wasn't coming back. Not just in his acid-wracked head, but for real. He just knew something else was coming – a big python coiling around him, the croc dragging him into the creek, a falling branch crushing his head, or maybe a giant wave rolling in from Japan.

It felt like the island had something more to throw at him, another test to see if he really wanted the prize. But he'd got away, a bit bloody battered, but in one piece. It might take a little longer to get over it mentally, though.

He could see now how people lost it for good on LSD. If it got bad, it got really bad. You needed peace and safety around you. He'd had that the first time, but the second time, what with everything that happened, was horrific.

It had been impossible to fight the badness, so he'd stopped fighting. But he hadn't given up – he'd accepted, and there was a big difference.

He left a note for Suzy – that he was taking Pep's boat again. The two briefcases of gold were burning a hole in Starcraft. He'd been too much of a vacant lot yesterday, but he needed to put them back in the ground for a while. Ideally in a spot behind a beach with no road leading in. Like where he'd found them. But without the dead people.

He didn't feel like driving too far just yet, so he went back into Cairns. At the Marlin Jetty, he'd get more fuel for the boat, then he'd eat a double serve of hot chips with salt and vinegar in the sunshine while he worked out which beach he'd go bury the cases on.

In town, he pulled into the jetty car park and looked across Trinity Inlet. Thirty or so yachts and boats were anchored by the mangroves on the other side, and among them he saw a flash of orange.

Damning that evil bastard for wrecking his binoculars, he got out and walked over to the water. He hadn't really thought consciously about it, but he knew now that he'd come here for more than fuel. Though hundreds of metres away, there was no doubt about it – the orange hull out there was the same tone as the yacht he'd seen at Zoe Bay.

Suddenly cold, he looked around. A big sugar carrier was cruising in towards the terminal. Yelling kids were jumping off the jetty into the sea. On the boat ramp, a man and a boy were winching a boat up onto a trailer. And the world was full of demons passing as men, fiends who took and discarded lives with careless ease. Murderman had come to Cairns.

He went back to the truck. Plans and ideas tumbled around his head. He could get a gun and some backup; Robbie's mad mate Simon sprang to mind, but it might take a day or two to organise, and then what – shoot them on their yacht in the inlet? He wouldn't mind that, but the sound of gunfire would make it very risky. He'd go to jail.

A good citizen would go to the cops, but somehow he knew that making accusations that Murderman and his mates would deny wouldn't work. It would be his word against theirs.

He could show the cops the motive, the gold, but he had a strong feeling it wouldn't be enough to convict anybody. Especially if there were no bodies. He'd be a suspect then, and who the hell knew what might happen to the gold? Things vanished from cop shops in far north Queensland all the bloody time.

He looked across the inlet at the orange yacht. He clenched his fists. Bugger this five ways, he thought. I need a clever move, but my brain's been double-dipped in LSD. Every choice involved planning and time he might not have. The yacht could up and go at any moment. The bastards would have arrived yesterday, cleared customs, and then resupplied. Now they'd be ready to sail away, never to be seen again.

He took a slow, deep breath. Breathed out. He was over feeling scared. He'd had a gutful of it. He got in his truck and backed the trailer down the boat ramp. He got the Starcraft into the water, tied it off, and then parked the truck.

Yeah, he'd go and have a look at the yacht. Drill a hole in its hull if necessary.

Shark Bait

Fifty metres from the shore, he let the motor idle while he had a look through Pep's gear. He found a tattered floral shirt, a pair of sunnies, and a filthy terry towelling hat and put them on. He'd slouch down in the bench seat to hide his height and play at being a Cairns yokel tooling around the inlet.

He needed to get close enough to see faces. If they were below deck, he'd give them a coo-ee to get them into the sunlight. With other boats close by, the odds of not getting shot felt pretty good. Then he'd work out what to do next.

Puttering along, he curved across the inlet until he was behind the orange yacht. He watched for movement. As he cruised in, he looked at the closest vessels, some not ten metres away, and was pleased to see a bloke busy with a brush on a yacht's front deck and someone else at a bow rail a few yachts down.

Coming in nice and easy behind the yacht, he saw its port of registry – San Francisco. No surprise there. Near the mangroves, he turned and went parallel to the green wall. Twenty metres away, he killed the engine. When the momentum stopped, he'd drift past on the outgoing tide.

A car horn sounded on the Esplanade. Water slapped gently on the Starcraft's hull. The stern of the yacht came closer. There was no one on deck. Ten metres, then five, still no signs of life. Time to play the fool and give them a hoy. He took a last look around, saw that the people on the other boats were still there. Good. Murderman and his mates would see them too.

Turning back, he saw someone in the companionway of the yacht: white t-shirt, yachtie brown skin, baseball cap, and looking down the barrel of a pistol at him. It wasn't a revolver, and it didn't move an inch.

The tide pushed the Starcraft closer. A face came out of the companionway shadow, the gun still rock solid.

A Yank voice said, "Oh God, I thought we'd killed you."

Seeing right through his disguise – Elinore.

Seth gripped the wheel hard. On the yacht, a breeze dinged the halyards against the mast.

"You gonna put that thing down?" He stood up, got the mooring line. She lowered the gun, engaged the safety, and put it on a shelf in the cockpit. The Starcraft bumped against the yacht. Seth reached out and caught the rail.

"I can't tell you how glad I am to see you," said Elinore, as she came across the deck to take the rope. Her face was shining with emotion. She tied off the Starcraft, and Seth hopped up onto the deck.

He looked at the cockpit shelf, saw a Colt .45. He heard those gunshots again: one-two, one-two, then one more.

Elinore came to him, grateful, astonished, jubilant too. She looked different, her hair trimmed, earrings glinting, and a ladies watch on her wrist. With a sob, she hugged him. He stood there feeling her against him, and after the last few days it felt like a reward.

"I'm so sorry," she said into his neck. "So, so sorry."

"Who is it?" yelled a voice from the cabin.

Seth began to extract himself. She quickly let go, looked

at him, and he saw that offer again – the 'drop everything and be with me' offer. Then her eyes changed, willing him to understand that things were working at another level now. He said nothing; he didn't move.

"It's Seth!" yelled Elinore, her voice suddenly high with excitement. There was silence, then Jack's wild yell.

"He got hurt," said Elinore to Seth. "He can't walk. His Achilles tendon was severed, and it got infected. He was treated at the hospital here; now he's on antibiotics. And bourbon. He's been drunk since yesterday."

"Tell that wild colonial boy to come down!" called Jack.

Something dark swam across Elinore's face: an angry intolerance at her circumstances and real displeasure at the voice from below.

"What the hell happened?" said Seth.

She looked at the inlet, then back at him. "I'm so sorry."

"Yeah, you already said that."

She blew air out through her lips, then gestured for him to lead the way down into the cabin. He glanced at the Colt pistol as he went down the wooden steps into the cabin.

It smelt new, the cabin split-level. First a galley with a four-place table, the fittings and cabinets gleaming, then down a few steps to the main area of the cabin that was replete with lounge-style sleeping berths on either side.

On one of the berths, Jack sat propped up on pillows, bare-chested in shorts with a bandage on his foot. He roared in triumph at the sight of Seth.

"Doc Tarzan! You made it!"

He also looked different; his hair cut short, his beard closely trimmed, the earring gone. He gestured for Seth to come over, something like tears glinting in his eyes. As

Seth approached, he held out his arms for a hug. Leaning down for Jack to put his arms around him, Seth thought of the hours they'd spent on the LSD. It was strange; he didn't have memories of it – he had feelings.

As Jack held him tightly, Seth looked through an open door into a sleeping berth in the bow. Bags and boxes lay tumbled together on the mattresses, and the cushions had been pulled out and were piled in a heap in a corner.

Sunlight pierced a porthole. On the shiny timber floor there was a line of powder. It looked like fresh sawdust. Then Seth saw the bright line of a cut in the timber cabinet work beneath one of the berths.

Jack sighed, his beard against Seth's face. He smelt of grog, tobacco, and old sweat. "Ohhh, man," he rumbled. Seth began to pull away, but Jack kept hanging on. It was great he felt that way, but it was getting stupid now.

He got free. Elinore was right there, adjusting a pillow at Jack's shoulder. She smiled at him and moved back.

"Well, ring the bells, why don't you?" said Jack, and he peered at Seth. "Got a bit scratched up, huh?"

"Wow, wow, wow, hey? I'll make coffee," said Elinore, laughing with relief. "I think I need some bourbon, too."

With another smile, she squeezed Seth's arm.

"This is something else," she said. "So, so good!"

She went to the galley. Seth quickly followed.

"Hey," called Jack. "Hey, what happened to you, man?"

At the stove, Elinore looked at Seth as he sat down at the galley table. Jack stared up from the cabin. Elinore measured water into the coffee maker, then added three spoonfuls of the stuff. She put the pot on the stovetop and lit the gas, her eyes firmly on the job at hand.

When she finally turned to him, Seth said, "Who were the fellas in the creek?"

She grimaced. "Bad men."

Seth heard the flick of a lighter from the cabin and smelt pipe smoke. Elinore got out two mugs and two tumblers, pumped water, then carefully rinsed and dried them. Steam rose from the pot; the acrid smell filled the air. Seth stood and went over to her.

"What happened?" he said. She turned and faced him.

From the lounge, Jack coughed. Elinore stared at Seth, and he knew she was wondering what to tell him.

He looked down at Jack. "Who was that crazy bastard who came after me?" Jack shrugged, raised his hands, but there was bullshit in his eyes.

"What happened to your tendon?" said Seth. "The crazy man do that to you?"

"Yeah – the fucker! I couldn't walk. Threatened to do the same to Eli."

"So you didn't have the Colt when they did that?"

"No. No, I didn't."

"They were Americans, right?'

"I dunno, man. I couldn't really say who –"

"C'mon! This yacht's got San Francisco on its stern."

"Man, there's lots of yachts with –"

"Jack, shut up," snarled Elinore.

Jack's eyes became slits. Seth now got the strong idea that a whole lot had unravelled between them in the last few days. Maybe even in the last few weeks.

He looked at Elinore. Her eyes were shut, her lips tight. When she opened her eyes, she kept them on the flame. The pot hissed with steam, bubbled, the smell of brewing overpowering. She turned the flame off and gave him a hostess's smile. "I can't remember. Do you take sugar and cream?"

"Cream?"

"Yes, I went to the supermarket. I can't tell you how good that was. So much better than Vila."

"Both," said Seth. "So you shot them, hey?"

Elinore opened a tiny fridge and took out a small carton of cream. "It comes from those hills above Cairns. I didn't imagine that in the tropics."

"I told you about the dairy industry up here, how the crocodiles used to eat the cows."

"That's right, you did."

"That's your gun, isn't it?"

"Yes," said Elinore. Jack groaned.

"So what happened?" said Seth.

"Coffee," she said. "Coffee first."

She poured the coffee, added sugar and cream, and with an encouraging smile nodded at Seth to get the tumblers. She went down to the cabin, and Seth followed. He sat down next to her on the berth facing Jack and put the tumblers on the timber armrest. As Elinore gave him his coffee, Jack held up a bottle of bourbon.

"A shot for the Doc?" he said. Seth shook his head.

"Say, you got any more of that weed, soldier boy?" said Jack. "I'm fucked up, but not fucked up enough."

"Mate, I'll just have my coffee first."

"Of course, man, of course. Be my guest."

Seth turned to Elinore. "Who were the dead fellas?"

"Two guys we knew in San Francisco. We sailed across the Pacific with them. We all left Port Vila together."

"Why did they attack you?"

"They knew I had some valuables onboard. How they found out, I don't know."

Blank-faced, Jack puffed on his pipe.

"Things felt weird in Vila," said Elinore. "When Joey and Robbie got off there after they'd crewed with us and Guthrie, I felt something coming. When we got separated in the storm, we came to Zoe Bay. I didn't think we'd get reported missing any time soon by them. I thought they'd go to Gladstone, then on to Sydney as planned. Or maybe Cairns. But no – somehow Guthrie chose Zoe Bay."

"Jesus, Eli, everyone's talked about Zoe," said Jack. "It wasn't a state secret. Not to them, not to us."

"You're going to have to shut up, or you're not going anywhere," said Elinore.

"What happened when they turned up?" said Seth.

"They came ashore, and we talked on the beach, then we went to the camp," said Elinore. "Guthrie said nothing about us being six hundred miles further north than expected, but he was holding a shirt, and he dropped it next to Jack. There was a knife in it, and when he went to pick up the shirt, he cut Jack's tendon."

"Sneaky fuckin' rat," said Jack. "While I was standing there talking to him."

"Larry grabbed me," said Elinore, "and Guthrie gave him the knife to hold at my throat, and he went and got your pack. He knew it wasn't ours. He took your machete and hit me with the flat of it on my ass and legs."

Jack swore bitterly.

"I didn't want to say anything, but he began hacking at the sand around Jack's head. I said we'd just met you and that you must have gone for a walk. I'm so sorry."

"Fuckin' fucker," snarled Jack.

"He told Larry to cut Jack up if I tried to run. Then he went off after you." Elinore looked at the low timber roof.

"What happened with Guthrie?" said Jack. "You hurt him, right? He was limping good, but he never said shit."

"Who was Guthrie?" said Seth.

Jack shook his head, sucked air through his yellowed teeth. "A really bad motherfucker."

Seth had never heard anyone say that before.

"You fight him?" said Jack eagerly. "You bust his foot?"

Seth nodded.

"But he had your machete," said Jack.

"Yeah. It's made of Port Kembla steel."

Jack laughed with something like awe. "But he couldn't get you, huh? The Aussie Vietcong."

You heard of the Green Berets? Seth remembered the question from what felt like a hundred years ago. *Long-range reconnaissance, hit and run ambushes.*

He turned to Elinore.

"So why were you mixed up with this bastard?"

Elinore sighed. "He was just a guy. Jack met him in the yachting scene. Everyone knew he'd been in Vietnam, that he'd seen the light and come back a changed man. We have to forgive and forget, right? He liked dope and rock music and sailing. He had a job and a house. He seemed like an upright guy."

"Sure suckered me," spat Jack.

"And the other bloke?" said Seth.

"Good on a boat, but a hoodlum really," said Jack.

"Larry was okay until he wasn't," said Elinore.

"Slimy cock-sucking bastard," said Jack, sitting up. "I would have shot him down for what he did to you."

Elinore closed her eyes, quietly made a fist. Wide-eyed, Jack licked his lips, and she continued.

"Jack and Larry and Guthrie had a boys' drinking club – shut up, Jack – and we sailed with them and other friends around the Bay, along the coast, and down to Baja California. Festivals, concerts, parties – they were part of the gang. We sailed to Hawaii last year. It was all cool."

"Did they have a gun?" said Seth.

"A rifle. But they left it on the yacht, thank God."

"How did you . . . do it?" said Seth.

"You sound like a fucking cop with all these questions," said Jack.

"After the shit you bastards put me through, I think I deserve to hear what happened," said Seth.

Elinore looked at Jack, and he sat back on the pillows.

"I brought the Colt with us when we first came ashore," she said. "Hid it behind a log near the camp. In a plastic bag. Jack couldn't walk, and Larry said he'd hurt him bad if I ran and that Guthrie would find me. But I wasn't going to run with just one of them there. So we waited, Jack shouting and swearing at Larry. I felt terrible that we'd got you caught up in this, but I knew you'd make it."

"I'm glad someone did," said Seth.

"When Guthrie finally got back, I saw his foot was hurt."

"He have the machete?" said Seth.

"Yes, he did. I didn't like it when he came in under the trees with it. He was limping, looking mad as hell, and I ran for the gun. They came after me like dogs."

Seth saw the elation the memory stirred in her.

"I grabbed it, tore the bag off as I ran to the creek. When I turned, Larry was right there, hands out to grab me. I shot him twice. As he fell, I lined up on Guthrie."

She smiled. "He couldn't believe it. A woman, too."

"A third bullet for him, hey?" said Seth.

"Oh yeah."

Seth flashed on the creek at Zoe Bay, the pale sunlit skin among the dead black leaves, the granules and shreds of pink and red gently moving in the crystalline water.

"Daddy would be proud of me," said Elinore. "He might be rich, but he didn't shirk his duty fighting the Nazis. He taught my brothers and me how to shoot, my mother too. He doesn't like weakness. Especially in women."

Daddy's one smart bastard, thought Seth.

"What happened to Vicarious?" he said.

"The next morning we towed it out past the headland and scuttled it. We couldn't manage two yachts, and this was the better boat."

"Why leave the next morning? Why not straightaway?"

"We waited for you."

Seth heard a sudden click, Jack's teeth on his pipe stem.

"And Jack was in shock. Lots of shock."

The pipe crackled. Elinore waited, her eyes on Seth.

Seth nodded slowly. "So, how did it go with the hospital and customs?"

"Fine. I radioed in, and there was an ambulance at the jetty. Everyone was so helpful at the hospital. I think we were the excitement on what looked like a slow, hot day."

"And customs?"

"They came out and did the paperwork, stamped our passports, inspected the boat. It took half an hour, if that."

What about logbooks? thought Seth. Crew lists?

Of course she knew what he was thinking.

"Both yachts were on their maiden voyage. New fittings, new logbooks. Both owned by a company. My company."

"A company now with one yacht and no fuckin' crew," said Jack. "It was heartbreaking putting Vicarious down. If you'd been there, we might have got them both out."

Elinore made a cutting motion with a hand. Jack shut up. They sat in silence, Elinore looking at Seth. Across the water in town, a shunting train in the rail yards banged in metallic cacophony.

"So, what are the chances of me not ending up in an Australian jail?" said Elinore.

"Pretty good," said Seth.

She looked at him like he was the smartest fella on two legs. It was strong medicine.

"Well, thank you, Seth. I really owe you."

"Why the LSD?" said Seth.

"We liked you, man," said Jack. "You shared your weed. We had a whale of a time, right? We connected, man."

They knew that would happen, thought Seth.

"Both of you asked me for help that night. Was this what it was about? Guthrie?"

Elinore looked levelly into his eyes.

"I didn't know what might happen, but I did not expect that," she said. "And to happen so soon."

"You should have asked me straight out," said Seth.

Elinore looked at Jack in angry vindication.

"It's easy to say now," said Jack. "But people say things when they're tripping they'll never do. And he might have gone to the cops. Shit, we don't know him from Adam."

Up your arse, thought Seth. Jack's insinuation cut him to the quick. They'd taken LSD together. They'd been like brothers. And he'd told them about himself and his family in Cairns. He'd been honest, open, and, damn it, he was a man of his word. He was a good bloke!

"Just because you're a nice guy doesn't mean you can't be a bad guy," said Jack.

"Jack, fucking can it." Elinore turned to Seth.

"Okay, I'm asking now. I need your help."

"Doing what?" said Seth, but he knew.

"I want you to go back to Zoe Bay with us."

"It's not a good place to be anymore," said Seth.

"Did someone see you there?"

Seth thought about the question, then shook his head. He wasn't going anywhere with them.

"We'll pay you," said Elinore.

"To do what?" said Seth.

"To help us cover our tracks there."

Seth flashed on his souvenirs: the white plastic rabbit and the .45 shell.

"Those two assholes is what she means," said Jack.

"A thousand dollars US," said Elinore.

"We need another person," said Jack. "I'll tell you what to do. It'll be easy, man. We just need two hands on deck. With this ankle, I nearly killed myself taking Vicarious for her last ride."

He took a slug of his glass, his eyes slits in his bearded face. "I'll keep an eye out for crocodiles."

Seth said nothing. He wasn't going to tell them about the storm flushing out the creek either.

Seconds ticked past, and the expectation on their faces

hardened into tight smiles. Elinore flashed Jack a look he didn't acknowledge. He picked up the bourbon bottle and waggled it at Seth. "Ready for one now?"

This was man-to-man, acid-brothers style; not pushing it, just being loose and cool. Seth could play along with that. He took the bottle, uncapped it, and swigged hard. Surprised, Jack grinned at him uncertainly.

"You got any more weed, man?" he said. "For my pain."

Seth took another slug of bourbon. For his pain.

"Sure," he said. "But what happened to my machete? Guthrie had it when he came back, yeah?"

For a split second, Elinore's eyes went to the doorway of the front cabin. Jack surfaced a look of puzzlement.

Seth capped the bottle and put it on the floor. He held out his hand to Elinore. "Can I have it back, please?"

She looked at him, seeking intent, then smiled brightly. "Yeah, sure. I'll get it."

She went into the cabin. Jack stared at Seth like he was a pirate boarder who'd just come over the side. Behind him, Seth watched Elinore stretching across a berth. Jack smiled like he had the Colt in his hand. Elinore came out of the cabin and passed him his Machet 15.

He quickly stood, the blade dangling by his leg. Supine, Jack twitched, like his hand was moving under the sheet. Elinore's face went blank. The cabin grew small. Standing there, Seth thought about it.

Crossing the Pacific Ocean in this? Week after week, month after month. Down for days in the cabin when the weather was bad? You'd go bananas.

He waggled the Machet in the air. "Thanks. I'll go put it in my boat now."

Jack sniggered meanly; Elinore smiled serenely. Seth went up top, and as he crossed to the rail, he heard voices rise in forceful tones, Elinore's dominant.

Hopping into the Starcraft, he undid the tarp. He put the Machet into its sheath on the slashed-up rucksack, then dug out the smoking tin. He paused, looked around. A pattern of serried clouds hung above the jungle green of the Lamb Range. In the big car park next to The Pacific Hotel, where The Strand had once stood, dust rose as some vehicles drove out.

He could quietly untie the boat now and take off with the two cases. Justify it as payment for what they'd put him through.

Or he could just admit to outright thievery like his brother Alex would – *We ripped 'em off because we're smarter than they'll ever be, and if they're gonna let themselves be fucked, then fuck 'em!*

Seth put the tin in his pocket. He could leave them in the dust here, ride the Bruce to Brissie, and disappear down the east coast. Sure, the Yanks would find the empty hole at Zoe, and they'd know it was him, but they'd be real shy about going to the cops about their undeclared goods, wouldn't they?

It would mean leaving Cairns for a good while. Years, maybe. He'd have to lie to his family and fend off his brother, as the bastard could sniff out a dollar anywhere.

But he'd told them too much about himself, and what if he was wrong about them not going to the authorities? Elinore was tough and smart; she had money – and a gun-toting father. What if they set American lawyers and state cops on him? The bastards would harass Mum and Dad.

From the airport came the sound of an aircraft taking off, and Seth listened to the rising drone, waiting for the consent to come. It didn't, and he got back on the yacht.

In the smoky cabin, the smell giving him the shits now, Seth gave Jack the tin. In silence, the Yank began rolling a joint, the unanswered question floating in the air. No one was going to push it. That's how much they wanted it.

Elinore smiled softly, her carefully vacant eyes on the cabin windows, like that's what you did on a yacht when you weren't talking to each other.

Jack lit the joint. Seth began counting in his head until Elinore finally said, "Are you in? A thousand dollars. US."

"To do what exactly?" said Seth. "I need details, or I'm not going anywhere."

"Sure, sure," said Jack. "Whatever you want to know. After tripping with you, man, I feel we have an affinity. We'll do this easy."

"Yeah, that's cool, but the details," said Seth.

"Okay, we rope them by the heels, bring 'em out to the yacht, re-tie 'em and head out to deep water."

"Like shark bait," said Seth.

Jack stared at him, then barked with laughter. "Yeah, like fucking shark bait."

"And dump them."

"Yeah. Cut the rope like ten or fifteen kilometres out."

"Then what?"

"We go back and . . . clean up."

"There's nothing to clean up."

"There could be," said Elinore.

Seth took the .45 shell out of his pocket and tossed it to her. She caught it and saw what it was.

"You *are* handy," she said, looking at him with naked admiration.

"So we dump the two blokes out in a channel and then leave? Is that it?" said Seth.

"There's something else," said Elinore.

"Drugs?"

"Oh, I've got some acid, but no. This is personal stuff I didn't want Guthrie getting his hands on or sending to the bottom of the ocean."

Jack worked the joint, his head a grey and white cloud. Some of the smoke disappeared up through the open top hatch; most of it swirled around the cabin. Seth stood up.

"Sorry. I'm smoked out down here. I gotta go up top."

He turned and went up to the back deck. Seconds later Elinore appeared, and she came and stood close to him.

"It's a lot to take in, I know," she said. "I'm so sorry that this all . . . exploded into your life. I didn't know Guthrie and Larry would do anything like that. It must have been horrible."

"Aww, yeah," he said. "Just another bad motherfucker."

Elinore laughed. Seth liked the awe in her voice.

"You're a hell of a man," she said.

He supposed he was.

"So, are you going to help me?" she said.

Seth thought about stringing her along a bit more, but he was tired of playing games. The fun of it hadn't lasted long. He climbed over the rail into the Starcraft.

"Wait! Seth, wait," said Elinore. "Please."

Seth undid the corners of the tarp and looked up at her.

"I didn't just find brass," he said. Pulling back the tarp, he dragged one of the black plastic cases into view.

Elinore's hands shot to her mouth and sealed it. Her knees came together. She stared in shock at the case. Seth pulled out the second one. Over her cupped hands, her big eyes grew huge.

Well, howzat, thought Seth. I just knocked your clever American arse for six. No, make that a ten.

She took her hands away, and her face was a collision of emotions: astonishment, gratitude at his honesty, pure lust, and something else. It was like he'd come through for her, that he'd made the grade.

She hopped the rail into the Starcraft, and threw herself into him, hugging close, her thighs on either side of his leg, her face snuggling under his jaw.

"Let's not blow this," she whispered into his neck. "Let's . . . let's see what we have here."

Seth felt her lips moving on his neck.

"This is meant to happen. I know you feel that. Let's go with it, follow it. The universe is joining us."

He pulled her arms away, extracted his thigh.

"Hop back onboard, and I'll pass 'em to you," he said.

She stared at him, her eyes flat, her mouth a tight pink line. Turning from her, he lifted the first case onto the brace of the Starcraft, then up to the yacht's deck. Then he tipped it with a thump to lay flat onto the deck.

Elinore looked at him, then got back onto the yacht. She pulled the case away from the rail, collected the second one as it came up, and then waited as Seth retied the tarp.

Done, he got on board the yacht. She looked at him like he was a specimen in a zoo, like she needed to remember the command that would make him dance or swing from a tree. He picked up a case. "After you," he said.

She picked up the other one, biceps firming, and walked to the companionway. Straddling the case, she lugged it down the steps. She began laughing, something hard and sharp in her voice.

"Lookee here! It's all here! Doc Tarzan brought it with him! Lookee here!"

Seth heard Jack swear in disbelief. As he brought the case into the cabin, Elinore watched him as though he was the whitest of white knights, living proof of the inherent goodness in man. She pealed with mad laughter again, loving him with her eyes, then went to Jack. She grabbed his shoulder and laughed some more, her eyes on Seth. Pipe clenched in one hand, Jack stared at him.

"What a good man you are, Seth," said Elinore. "I am so, so lucky. Aren't I, Jack?"

Jack plastered on a smile.

"You heard me digging," he said to Seth.

Seth nodded. "Yeah, I did."

The Yank twisted on the bed like he was in pain.

"Oh man, that's unfortunate," he said, and he brought the Colt up and aimed it at Seth's chest.

"Go up to the galley, babe," he said to Elinore.

"For God's sake, Jack," said Elinore, but she quickly went towards the galley.

Seth could have grabbed her as she passed, but he knew this was a movie, and after the craziness on the island, he wasn't going to get too worried about it.

Hopalong Cassidy sat there sweating, holding the gun.

"Are you that stupid, mate?" said Seth. "You fire that cannon, and a hundred people will come and see what the racket's about, including the cops and the navy just across the inlet. You got a jetpack to get away?"

He stared at the idiot, trying to reconnect with the bloke from the island, the cool American, his friend. But all he saw was an angry and humiliated man flying on booze and painkillers and stumped by his injury.

Jack stared back, and with a flip of the guts, Seth saw that this wasn't really about gold and dead men and keeping his mouth shut, big as all that was. It was a lot more primitive than that. Jack thought he was going to take his woman and get everything he had going with her.

This Australian bastard was the new model: younger and proven. He'd fought the bad man and brought back the gold. Now he'd claim the real prize. And after Elinore's carry-on up top just then, Seth wasn't entirely sure he was wrong.

"How many blokes have you shot?" he said.

"You'd be surprised," said Jack.

"Bullshit."

The yachtie glared with mad eyes and bared teeth. He looked like a wounded animal awaiting a final bullet.

"I would have shot Guthrie if he hadn't cut me," he said.

"Maybe," said Seth. "But the chaperone took care of it, didn't she? Whose idea was it to bring the Colt ashore?"

"Mine," said Elinore.

"Well, there you go," said Seth.

"Okay, let's stop this now," said Elinore. She came back through the cabin, her hip brushing Seth's arm in passing.

She went to Jack, stood over him, her bikini bottoms and long brown legs blocking Seth's view.

"Give it to me," she said, her voice firm and calm.

Jack rasped and muttered. She listened, then replied in

a low, hard voice. She bent forward, then straightened up. She turned around, the Colt in hand. She looked down at the safety, and from the look on her face, it appeared it had been on the whole time. Behind her, Jack burped.

Elinore looked at Seth, her finger along the side of the trigger guard. Her eyes were flat and dark, her mouth set hard. She looked like the poster for a film he'd like to see.

"You tell anyone about what happened?" she said.

Oh man, thought Seth. I'm being monstered by a Yank chick in bikini pants holding a Colt 45.

"Yep," he lied.

He nodded towards the shore. "They're in the car park over there. Eating mango Weis bars."

"Mango Weis bars?"

"Yeah, they're real nice, aye."

"Hear that, Jack?" said Elinore. "His friends are here."

With a brittle smile, she lowered the gun to her side and went past him, her smooth belly at eye level, little ringlets of dark hair escaping the edges of her bikini.

"How fucked up would that have been, Jack?" she said over her shoulder. "How fucking dumb, hey?"

Hang about, thought Seth, you gave him the gun. While he was hugging me.

Up in the galley she squatted and opened a cupboard. Jack lay brushing his beard with a claw-like hand, his hot, mad eyes fixed on Seth.

Elinore stood, hands empty. She took a cloth shopping bag off a hook and put it over her shoulder. Picking up one of the black cases, she lugged it down to the cabin and put it on the floor between the lounge berths.

"I need to open that," she said, motioning at a drawer

between Seth's legs. He stood and got out of the way. She got on her knees and slid open the drawer. Both men watched her as she took out a big sketchpad and opened it to a sheaf of clear plastic sleeves. Removing one, she put everything back in the drawer and closed it.

She cracked the case and gave the contents a good look. Jack worked on his pipe, tapping and gouging. Elinore looked up at Seth with more starry-eyed wonder and awed appreciation in her eyes. She looked absolutely ready for anything. With a fairy godmother smile, she put a gold bar in the cloth bag. The tapping stopped.

"What are you doing?" Jack's voice cracked in outrage.

She turned to him with an awful face, her whole posture filled with overwhelming intent to negate and silence him.

"Shut the fuck up!"

She gave him death-ray eyes. Jack stared back, his brow a scrape of pain.

"You are *just* about out of chances," she said.

She turned back to her gold and put another five bars in the bag. Seth saw the pleasure she got doing it, of being the one who *could* do it, and he realised what that power he'd seen in her was. Money. And lots of it.

Opening up the satchel of art books, she took one out. Holding it by the corner, she took one of the sheets of blank white paper from between the pages and carefully slid it into the clear plastic sleeve. She held it out to Seth, and he took it.

"Keep this dry and cool and out of the sunlight," she said. "Cut it into two hundredths. Use a ruler and a sharp blade."

Seth looked at the paper in the sleeve.

"Acid," said Elinore. "Blotter paper. Two hundred drops at two hundred and fifty mikes each."

"Acid," said Seth.

Now he remembered how he'd run his fingers down every sheet of the paper and then repeatedly rubbed his eye with his fingers, trying to ease the incessant itch the stink bug had caused. Jesus.

"It's what you had. Share it with special people. Turn on the good and great," said Elinore. "People like you."

She took the plastic sleeve and put it in the bag with the gold, then looked at him with appraising eyes, like all he had to do was take one little step. But all or nothing.

But he wasn't sure he wanted it all. His honesty had earned him a nice little reward, thank you, ma'am, but the smoke in the cabin was killing him.

He picked up the bag and stood. Jack made a strangled noise and showed his teeth in a rictus of relief.

"Well, our boy's paid off," he said. "I guess he's done."

"Yep," said Seth.

"Those two cases are going into a bank vault, man," said Jack. "We ain't keeping them on the boat. You can tell your buddies that."

Seth shrugged and began to turn.

"Wait." Jack looked pretty stoned now, his face gone sloppy and sincere. "Listen, man. Seth. I'm really sorry that things turned out so rough. That's not how we usually sail."

Somehow Seth didn't believe him.

Then, in solid proof of the mind's resilience, his memory found the quote, the thing that had struck him as so cold in White Fang.

"There were the eaters and the eaten," he said. "The law was: eat or be eaten."

Recognition blurred Jack's face. "What ya say?"

Elinore stood and walked up to the galley. Seth nodded at Jack and followed her up out onto the deck. She stood in the sunlight, her hands on the curve of her hips.

"Good quote," she said. "It feels like a real affirmation of what I was forced to do."

Seth went past her to the Starcraft, leaned over, and put the cloth bag on the bench seat.

"Good old Jack London," said Elinore, coming over.

Seth watched her lean on the rail and casually tuck a hand down the front of her bikini pants.

"It doesn't have to end here," she said. "Things change. Sometimes fast."

Seth got a flash of Jack going over the side somewhere remote and quiet. Shark bait. Her hand moved across her flat brown tummy and idly played with a curl of dark hair.

Seth blinked. He *was* the new model. She was offering him a big future, the money and acid wrapping it up in a bow. This was a chance to be in a movie, a movie where the pirates wore bikini bottoms, took LSD, and gave fellas gold bars. His part was to be consort to the queen, a real handy one, too. And he'd get to shoot the Colt.

With her, he'd blast off into the stratosphere and leave the far north far behind. A good few blokes would jump at the offer, his brother at the head of the queue, but this all felt desperate to him and filled with ill portent.

At the speed she went, he'd always be in her bow wave, with every shot being called from ahead. With two men down and an injured boyfriend in tow, she was on the back foot, and he'd never liked being with chicks like that. And who knows when the next new model might come along?

He shook his head, and she smiled sweetly like she'd never put a bullet in a bloke.

"Nothing I can do to convince you?" she said.

It was stupid how tempting it was. A real stroking of his ego. Any doubts about how dangerously cool he might be were gone. This woman from America had nailed that.

"I go fast, I know. Sorry," said Elinore. "Look, I got you the moment we met. Everything happens for a reason."

That last line gave Seth real pause. When she'd 'cleaned up' at Zoe she'd left his rucksack behind. Then another thought struck him. What exactly had she told Guthrie about him?

But he didn't want to think about it, and he turned from her and climbed over the rail into the Starcraft.

"So that's it?" said Elinore. "Back to wrangling drunks when the gold runs out."

"Probably not," said Seth, thinking of his mate Robbie the Bomb. "We got gold that grows on trees up here."

She stared at him, then cried out in alarm.

"Oh God, I forgot," she said. "Guthrie and Larry! We have to do something about them."

Seth undid the mooring rope.

"Listen, Seth, please! We have to do like Jack said. We have to get those bodies out to sea."

Seth pushed off. Her voice became desperate.

"I'll double the gold. Look, I just *gave* it to you – what about doing something in return? Huh?"

Firing up the Evinrude, he got the hell out of there.

Good As

At Spence Street he waited for the train to pass, the tray of the ute in front bristling with dogs. Chains rattled on steel as they eagerly went from one side to the other. They looked hale and hearty, and Seth was pleased about that. Blokes who didn't look after their dogs, or any animal for that matter, were less than human in his estimation.

On the other side of the tracks, he went south along the railway line where empty cane bins sat in long rows in the sun. Just past the showgrounds and racetrack, he turned left into Buchan Street and entered a warren of streets: timber workers' cottages up on poles, tin-roofed sheds, shabby workshops, and yards stuffed full with old vehicles and parts of vehicles, scavenged building materials, and stacks of old tyres.

This was Bungalow, the old suburb tucked in at the edge of the creeks and swamp that formed the indelible south-eastern boundary of Cairns. Not far from the CBD, it was pretty much the arse-end of town: the wrong side of the tracks, and then some. Bounded on three sides by creeks –Alligator, Chinaman, and Smiths – parts of Bungalow in the wet stunk like a drop toilet. King tides and standing water brought flocks of mozzies, and back during the war years, hundreds had died of malaria around here.

He took a turn, then another, driving down towards the swamp. In the distance, the Murray Prior Range was free of cloud, the gas tanks looking stark and modern against the jungle hills. He passed creeper-draped chain-link fences, mouldering caravans, peeling demountable sheds, and rusted shipping containers.

Cairns was small, but he didn't come down to this part of Bungalow much. In fact, maybe never. But he was here to do the right thing. He'd done the right thing on a yacht on the inlet the other day, and it had got a gun pointed at him – twice. Here in little old Bungalow, he wasn't sure if he'd be any better received.

The bloke would be ropeable; you could say that was a given. He might get stroppy, and Seth might get punched. But it had to be done. He had no idea how it would go, but he was here in peace. No matter what happened.

Once again he'd been hooked by his brother's bullshit. He should have ignored him, done nothing, but he didn't want the bastard and his mates, the Macs, thinking he was weak. He had a reputation to maintain. Start looking soft, and every bastard would think they could have a go at you.

Then realisation flowered in his mind, and he saw the whole reputation performance for what it was: blokes playing mind games rooted in biffo and intimidation, monstering each other and revelling in notoriety; fools all competing to be the top dog, with everybody having to hit someone eventually to prove how tough they were.

Well, bugger that. It was kid's stuff. He couldn't give a rat's arse anymore if people thought he was a hard nut or not. After Hinchinbrook he knew how tough he was, and that's all that mattered.

He saw the dirt road he was looking for. With a wall of guinea grass on one side and some scabby tin sheds on the other, it ended at a grove of trees by the swamp. He pulled onto the rutted grass strip by one of the sheds. Two cars, a Holden and a Ford, were parked on a gravel pad, and in the driveway, to his relief, was a red Monaro.

He got out, wrinkling his nose at the mangrove stink blowing in from the inlet. He looked across the swampy floodplain to the sugar wharf, then flinched as an insect buzzed past his face.

As he went towards the open side of the shed, Rory Wales came out, a beer in his big hand. He looked at Seth in surprise, then turned and yelled back into the shed.

"Hey, Freddy! Nonga! Get out here!"

Two blokes, stubbies in hand, came outside. Big boys, they looked to be mates from Rory's footy team, and they stared at Seth like he was the ball.

"Well, knock me down with a D12. It's Seth Kelly; come over to get his fuckin' block knocked off," said Rory.

The boys put their beers against the tin wall of the shed. Rory, eyes ablaze, took a last swig, then bounced his can off a forty-four-gallon drum.

"G'day, Rory," said Seth.

"G'day my arse," said Rory, and the three men strode forward.

Seth held up a chunk of sunshine – a piece of gold bar. Rory and his mates stopped, staring at the blaze of light.

"This is for hitting you," said Seth. "I was wrong. I found that out later, but it doesn't excuse it."

"Yeah?" said Rory, eyes wide in surprise as they flicked between Seth and the gold. "I told you, didn't I?"

"You did. And I didn't listen. I sincerely apologise, and I'm more than sorry that your mum and dad were there."

He held out the gold. "This is to say I mean it."

Looking a bit shocked, Rory came forward and took the gold. Seth let him play with it, feel its weight.

"So, we all square now?" he said.

Rory looked up, his face relaxed.

"Yeah, mate, we're square."

"Wait a sec, Rory," said one of the boys. "Isn't this the bastard who thumped you outside the church?"

"The very same," said Rory with a laugh.

The penny dropped, and the boys nodded and grinned. Well, how was this for a turn-up? What had seemed like a flogging in the making was now a win for their mate. The bastard had come back to say sorry – and with some gold too. It was a hell of a story!

With an open-mouthed grin, Rory examined the lump of metal in his hand. His mates chuckled and chugged on their beers. Rory looked up, eyes bright with memory.

"So, how was this bastard's form?" he said, nodding at Seth. "He came right into the church. I saw him standing there like the devil himself! How's that for real cheeky?"

He roared with laughter, and everyone joined in, Seth the loudest.

"Beer, mate?" said Rory as the hilarity died down.

"Thanks, but I'm gonna get going. Got a bit of a drive."

Rory looked disappointed. It wasn't every day a tough bastard came and apologised to him.

"Fair enough," he said. "Where you off to?"

"Down to Cardwell, then over to the Brook Islands."

"Jeez, that's a long way to go for a fish."

"There's a girl."

Rory and his mates sniggered.

"Long way to go for a bit of that," said Rory.

"Ah, not really," said Seth. "She likes fishing and drives the boat. Knows how to use a speargun, and she likes a drink too. She's a real good sort."

There was a massed groan of appreciation.

"I'll pick her up from the resort, and we'll camp on one of the islands. There's a beaut little sand spit there. Come sunset tonight, we'll be cooking fish and having our first rum."

Rory and the boys looked almost teary-eyed.

"Mate," said Rory. "Sounds like heaven."

"I reckon," said Seth.

A soundtrack to Heaven & Hell

Here are some tracks that speak of the story, the place, and era – the times, latitude, and attitude.

Slipstream – Sherbert
Spiders & Snakes – Jim Stafford
Swamp Man – Martha Velez (feat. Paul Kossoff)
Frankenstein – Edgar Winter Group
The Song of the Wind – Santana
Obscured by Clouds – Pink Floyd
Paper Mountain Man – Linda Perhacs
Spray – Can
Watch the Sunrise – Big Star
Jump Into The Fire – Harry Nilsson
Commando Line – Stevie Wright
Fire & Brimstone – Link Wray
The Bad Will Die – Keith Mlevhu
Up North – Catherine Howe

Acknowledgements

Massive thanks to my beta readers, especially
Tonya Whittaker & Craig Simons, for their
proofreading and error-spotting skills.

Big love and eternal gratitude to Jan Brown
for her savvy advice, continuing support, and
keen eye for both facts and emotions.

I also acknowledge the traditional owners and
custodians of Munamudanamy (Hinchinbrook
Island), where most of this book is set,
the Bandjin and Girramay people.

Author's Note

Far North Queensland is full of characters. Over the years, I've been lucky enough to meet a few of them. So, this is where I tell you that the resemblance to anyone living or deceased in this book is entirely coincidental.

A new Seth Kelly book, Learn to Run, will be out next year.

More on the series at **thecolourofshadows.com**